WHEN THE SNOW SETTLES

A *Lodge Affair* Novella

RACHEL LABERGE

Paperback ISBN: 979-8-9891308-3-2

Editing by Kay Morton and Kendra with Spice Me Up Editing.

Cover design by Love Lee Creative.

Letter from the author

Some readers feel some type of way when it comes to any extra information, including triggers or content warnings. I'm going to share those in the next paragraph. If you don't need them, turn the page. Quick. Now is your chance!

First and foremost, this novella is a continuation of *A Lodge Affair*. While it can be enjoyed as a standalone, you will have a more enriching experience if you read *A Lodge Affair* first. I did have both alpha and beta readers who approached this project without having read the first book, and they still found it enjoyable.

Now, let's discuss trigger and content warnings.

In *When the Snow Settles*, you may encounter descriptions of anxiety and panic attacks, grief, the mention of a sibling's death, references to a previous assault (including a brief flashback), explicit language, and on-page sexual content.

CHAPTER ONE
Ivy

I HOPE THE PERSON who argued with the flight attendant, caused a two-hour flight delay, and ended up on the no-fly list steps on Legos for the rest of forever. Naturally, the delay meant getting into the city during rush hour traffic—cue the two and a half hours sitting in the car that would've been avoided. I actually opted to walk the last few blocks because I'd rather trek with all my luggage instead of wasting another second in traffic.

After traipsing through fresh snow, the wheels to my suitcase covered in ice and salt, I finally make it to my apartment. I find the key and put it in the lock, like I've done a thousand times before. Pushing inside, I find the light switch, and am greeted with the familiar smell of lavender and the feel of home. It's almost just the way I left it, minus some of my most favorite things, which I packed up and moved to The Emerald Canopy Lodge. The things I couldn't be without are with Holland in Washington, and I'm here, in New York.

It's funny how things work out, huh?

"Earth to Ivy. Quit looking so wistful like your husband just went away to war," Vivian, my best friend and obsessive video-caller, interrupts my thoughts. "It's only for a few weeks. You'll be back out in the middle of nowhere with your grumpy lodge owner and howling French bulldog in no time," she jokes and rolls her eyes.

"Cut me some slack. Today was draining and it's a little weird being back here."

"At least you're in your old apartment and not posted up at a hotel. That would get old quick." I watch as she looks down at her freshly manicured nails.

"Yeah, I actually can't believe Stella really took over my rent."

Last year there was quite the scandal at Sparks Wellness, when one of my ex's, who was also a colleague, was found guilty of embezzlement, misappropriation of funds, and indecent exposure. Jack Wright is a complete slime ball—plus a horrific ex-boyfriend—and I'm thankful I'll never have to speak to him again. It's the least he could do after derailing a personal vacation with a work trip, putting me into a questionable situation with one of his dickbag friends, and cheating on me throughout our relationship.

After the dust settled from the trial, I told Stella, my boss, I wanted to move out west and work remote; she couldn't say yes fast enough. She even offered to take on my rent as a company expense, so I could stay in a familiar place a few times out of the year when I'd work in the office. I've made the trip three times but this is the first extended one: almost three weeks.

"Can you take yourself out of hyper planning mode and do coffee and yoga tomorrow morning?" Viv asks.

The only person who can get away with making fun of my severe attention to detail and preparedness is Vivian—the sister I never had. Literally. I'm an only child and in my adult life, my parents have caught the travel gene. I think they're somewhere near the Greek islands this week.

"As long as we stop at that new bakery," I sigh, acting like this would be difficult. Viv, a talented baker herself, is always my go-to when it comes to trying new food, especially anything including butter and sugar. She's one of the best parts of being back in New York.

"Already planning on it."

"Even if it's snowing! I need the vibes," I press. I know that Vivian hates the cold. She'd rather take a cab than walk any number of blocks in the winter.

"Fine. Even if it's snowing!" She blows me a kiss, after a very enthusiastic eyeroll and ends the video call.

I bring my roller bag to what used to be my bedroom and pause. The furniture is the same but that's about it. I made out like a bandit when Sparks bought out my lease; they also paid me for all of the furniture and décor I didn't want to bring with me to Washington.

My phone vibrates, bringing me back to the moment.

Holland-not-Tom

Slate is staring out the window

think he's waiting for you

Because the words aren't enough, a picture comes through. Slate, a gray French bulldog, is propped up on the loveseat, gazing out the window. I'm surprised he isn't howling—his favorite pastime when he doesn't get his way.

My eyes water as I look at the picture. It's weird to think how it wasn't too long ago when I didn't even know Slate existed; now he's cemented his fury self into my heart and soul. Jack was a whole lot of terrible, but if I hadn't worked at Sparks, dated that loser, and caught him having sex late at work, I wouldn't have made the solo-trip to The Emerald Canopy Lodge, where my entire world changed.

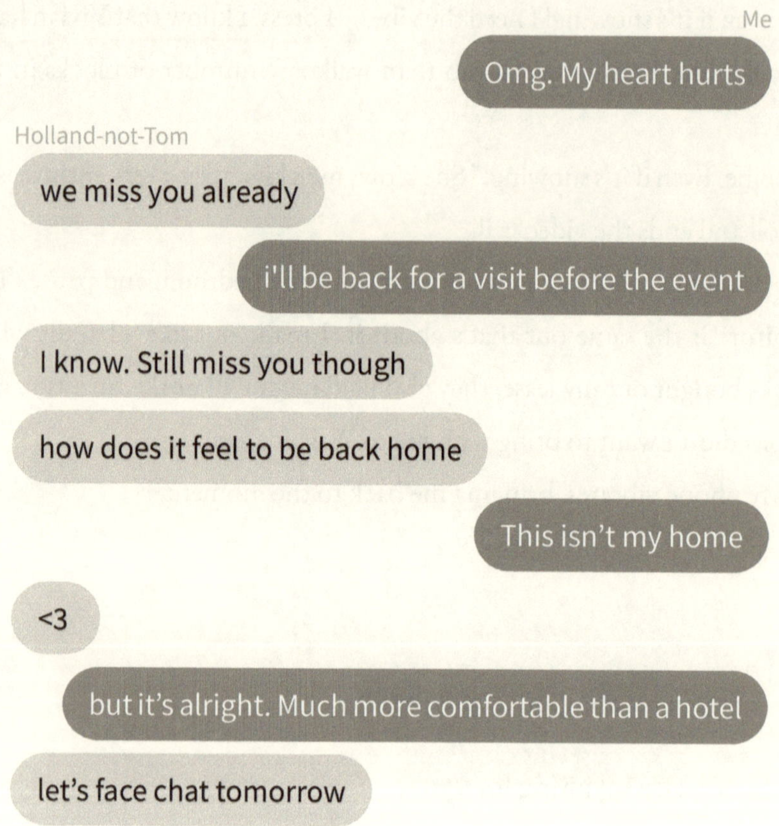

I smile at Holland using an emoji—also the term "face chat." The man is technology challenged, by choice, so the fact that his cell phone is even charged is a win. How things have changed, for both of us, since that fated day with my missing boxes for a client event at The Emerald Canopy Lodge.

There's nothing quite like not being able to find a bunch of boxes, with thousands of dollars of client items, and just as you're giving yourself the verbal beatdown of the ages, a handsome—but grumpy—lodge owner walks in with them. I'll never forget the first time Holland spoke to me with his casual, but so hot, "I'm guessing these belong to you?" His voice both rugged and velvety—a sound that's burned into my memory.

I owe my new life to those missing boxes. Now, there have been people who have flat out tried to make me feel bad about my choice insinuating I gave in and uprooted my city life for what a *man* wanted. People love to push their own insecurities onto others. It's not a secret I love the city—I always have—but being loved by someone like Holland gave me clarity on my love for the city. Maybe I needed the buzz, the constant feeling of something about to happen, because I didn't have someone I wanted to be still with.

Cheesy or not, it's the truth.

Holland and I text for a little while as I get settled. I unpack every single item from my suitcases and get myself comfortable. One of the many things therapy has taught me, and my uniquely wired brain, is that I feel best when I'm prepared, no matter the situation.

Therapy also reinforces how no one, not even me, can prepare for everything, but I'm still learning.

After unpacking groceries and stocking the fridge, I pull out the things I'm most excited for: a massive pad of sticky notes—I know just the place for it—and new markers. I open a closet door, greeted with a familiar creaking sound, and find the easel I hoped was still there. After wheeling it back to the kitchen, I pop the sticky notes on.

Is there anything better than a blank piece of paper?

My hands rest on my hips, touching the high-waisted leggings I can't get enough of—buttery smooth is an understatement. I shift my weight, back and forth, before taking the first piece of paper and sticking it to the wall. My fingers run along the edge, making sure it's secure and straight.

Typically, I wouldn't want work staring at me in the kitchen, but this is different.

I can't help but think back to the day when this whole project came to be.

A window pops up on my laptop: incoming Zoom call from Stella.

What? Why? There's nothing on my calendar. Oh god, am I getting fired? No, that doesn't make sense. But why else would my boss randomly ask for a Zoom meeting, at 4:30 PM on a Thursday?

My hand trembles on the track pad. I take a deep breath and click join, praying someone from HR isn't also in the waiting room.

"Ivy! I know you're probably spiraling but this is a good call. I promise."

I sigh out a breath that's audible to Stella on the other end, her hand on her chest, eyes compassionate and wide.

"You can't do that to me!" I say, my heart rattling in my chest.

"I thought I had this scheduled. That's my bad. I promise, you're not getting fired or anything like that." Her voice is level and clear, which is something I love about her. She takes my anxiety seriously and tries to support healthy boundaries.

"I've secured the funding from the board for a special event. I'm envisioning a red carpet, black tie situation."

"Ooooh, you know I love a red carpet." I shimmy my shoulders.

"We're thinking invite only, key clients plus celebrities and athletes, all in the hopes of raising some money. And brand awareness for Sparks."

This is the first I've ever heard of Sparks even considering something like this. My stomach flips in a good way—this sounds like fun.

"Which charity?" I ask, leaning my elbows on my desk and resting my chin on my hands.

"A 50-50 split. Ours and Yours is a non-profit focused on bringing mental health resources to high school and college students. Chin Up is for anyone impacted by sexual assault or domestic violence. They help people leave bad situations, as well as providing things such as self-defense classes," Stella explains.

Tears fill my eyes as Stella becomes blurry on the screen. She pauses, giving me the moment she knows I need. These charities are not random. Both topics are sewn into my being; they're both important in a way that I can't put into words.

Stella takes a deep breath and clasps her hands at her chest. "I'd like to formally offer you the lead position for the event. I know you'll have the heart, and the vision, to see this through in a way that these two organizations deserve." Her voice cracks a bit at the end.

I wipe a tear using the back of my hand. "Absolutely. I'd be honored."

"What kind of tears are these?" she asks.

Ha! Since I tend to cry more often than not, Stella has started asking me to categorize them. At first, it made me a little uncomfortable to answer but it's helpful to label them. And, if there's no words to describe, I say, "they're just tears."

"These are happy and grateful tears," I smile at the woman I'm proud to call my boss. There are so many people who hate their jobs and colleagues and I know I'm in the minority.

"This will require travel closer to the event and maybe a few weeks in New York, consecutively. Now that I have you on board, let's connect next week on details."

Here I am, in the homestretch of a project that's completely mine. We're so close, 24 days to be exact, and the excitement washes over me like the feel of a warm room when coming in from a cold winter day. The wave of anxiety quickly follows because I have to get this right.

If anyone can do this, I can.

Probably.

Hopefully.

CHAPTER TWO
Holland

"Do not feed him any more scones, Beatrice." I look over at Slate, licking his lips over and over, crumbs still on his snout.

Bea gasps, "Don't full name me!" She points at me, with her free hand, not the one about to give Slate another piece of scone. It did feel odd to say her full name, since she's known me since I was a kid, and she's worked at the lodge for as long as I can remember. I might be 36 years old but Bea keeps the upper hand like she always has.

Slate, the most spoiled French bulldog, whimpers and tilts his head—more effective than any type of puppy dog eyes.

My phone vibrates and I dig it out of my pocket. The lapse in attention has Bea throwing the last piece of peanut butter scone to Slate. I give her a side eyed look while opening my text messages: a selfie of Ivy and Vivian, eating donuts somewhere in the city. Ivy's wearing a smile that reaches her eyes. There's some sort of light in her face whenever she's with Viv. If she's not with me, I'm glad she's with someone like Vivian.

"How's our girl, Ivy?" Bea questions, petting Slate who is now in her lap.

"How do you know it's Ivy?"

"No one else makes you smile like that, one, and two, I don't think anyone else even has your phone number," she jokes.

But she's sort of right.

I snap a picture, less blurry than a typical first take, of Bea and Slate sitting outside at the lodge.

"Ivy says she loves you," I say to Bea before petting Slate's ears, "and you too." His soft gray blue fur is like velvet on my hands.

"How's New York?" Bea asks.

"Seems good and by that I mean chaotic, too many people, people who can't drive... typical."

"You're such a grump. You got the girl, and she lives with you out in the middle of the woods." She rolls her eyes. "You should be in a better mood."

It's not lost on me how much my life has changed since meeting Ivy. Definitely for the better. She's a force to be reckoned with, sometimes almost like my very own tornado. She whipped into my life like the quickest of summer storms, and honestly, I wouldn't change a thing.

Wait. That's a lie. I do wish she was here instead of across the country.

"I'm in a fine mood." I tell the lie I've told so many times.

I'm fine. Why does it feel like I can feel my jaw clench even when I'm just thinking about it?

This time, it's something completely different. Something unexpected.

"What are you even doing here? Today's your day off." Bea interrupts my thoughts, just in time.

"I own The Lodge. Do I need a reason?" I press, while looking around the mostly empty sitting area.

Sometimes my place is too empty, especially when Ivy is gone for work. The square feet is small and manageable but it's too quiet—it makes me miss her so much my chest hurts. Per my therapist, the pain is a physical manifestation of anxiety and missing Ivy.

I never went to therapy before meeting Ivy but I've learned a lot. For example, all the times I was feeling like my brain couldn't compute situations or everything was out of control when I was in public or large gatherings, was mostly undiagnosed social anxiety.

When I first started, I'd go once a week and dread getting out of my truck. Instead of scolding me for being late, my therapist would point out that she could see my truck in the parking lot, early, and she'd try to get me to understand why it was difficult to walk into the building.

Now, I see her once a month—prompt and on-time.

"You're the owner, but you now have a very competent general manager and staff who have everything under control."

She's right. I made the decision to hire a general manager last year and Mackenzie has been perfect. Giving up tasks is easier when someone who knows what they're doing is there to help. To be honest, Mackenzie hasn't let me down.

"Wildflower Fiction wants to do a popup event. I'm trying to figure out the best layout and brainstorming some sponsor ideas, things that will bring people here." I take in the spacious patio.

"Bailey! She's such a doll," Bea slaps her hands on her knees. "She has the best book recommendations, plus she gave me my smut for breakfast sticker I love so much."

I give her a side-eye look, "Smut for breakfast? What the hell is smut?"

Bea rolls her eyes like a dramatic teenager. "Smut. You know. Like sexy books." Bea shakes her shoulders, emphasizing the point.

I can't help but laugh. This is the same woman who signed guest room cards with LOL, thinking it meant lots of love. Now she's telling me about smut?

Since hiring Mackenzie, one of the funniest and most capable people I've crossed paths with in the employee sense, I get to work on, well, whatever the hell I want. Lately, I've been involved with small businesses in the community. So far, it's to give them the space to host events, which The Emerald Canopy Lodge has.

"Let me know how I can help with the pop up," Bea says, while setting Slate on the ground. "I'm headed back to the front office. Don't just lurk around here all day. Go do something." She puts her hand under my chin and then points at me, just like a parent would. Her eyes are on my mine, like she's waiting for me to say something.

I almost tell her my secret.

Almost.

But I don't.

I will, probably, but I need to wrap my head around this—figure out what I want.

CHAPTER THREE

Ivy

"Why would I order a *rice* sculpture? I didn't even know this is something that existed," I plead into the phone as I stare at a very detailed New York skyline sample sculpture that's outside of my office at Sparks Headquarters.

It's massive.

It's kind of blocking my door.

It's entirely made of rice.

It's mocking the lunch I skipped to accept the delivery.

The person on the phone finds my order, confirms it is supposed to be ice, and is trying to figure out what happened and how to get me a new sculpture to approve.

Colleagues snicker and cover their mouths when they see what I'm dealing with. I don't have the energy to hide my irritation and try to be positive since I'm rarely in the office and don't want to give anyone the wrong impression. The last of my patience and understanding just floated away the moment I realized another mistake had been made.

The last few days have been brutal. Wrong. Unpredictable. For someone who attempts to account for the expected, and any single thing that could go amiss, these days have been my nightmare.

In theory, the event is planned and we're getting to the end, but when it comes to execution, anything that could possibly come up has. Rice sculptures instead of ice sculptures, double invites being sent to some guests while others haven't received a single one, and the venue getting the time wrong for the event which led to a double booking.

A project that was once ahead of schedule yesterday is now drastically behind. I also am trying to build up the poor social media intern who just bursts into tears every time she sees me—per her explanation, she struggles with authority. She thrives on being perfect, giving me things before I ask for them, and knowing the answers. It's like she's a younger version of myself, but let's be real, I'm still an emotional human. I don't see that changing, ever, because no matter how much therapy I do or meds I take, I still cry about everything.

I'm afraid to move the cart it's set on, so I suck in my stomach and attempt to slink into my office. I drop my phone and try to catch it, which has me taking out the end of the sculpture. Rice is everywhere. My phone is drowning in rice.

The breath I sigh out in crippling defeat is hard to get back. My lungs are tight—there's no room for air. Pins, needles, and invisible knives dance on the top of my skin. The wave is expected but it's still somehow surprising. The anxiety and panic is hot. Unrelenting—like a bully you can't outrun.

I grab my phone from the smashed rice—cringing at that sensory experience—move the cart, and close my door. Grains of rice litter my floor and into the hallway.

As the door clicks, there's a light knock on the door.

"I need a minute," I scratch out, trying to keep it together.

"This is kind of an emergency." The small voice from Olivia, our very young social media intern, is barely audible.

She's young. She's standing in rice. She needs help. Your meltdown can wait.

I open the door, gathering myself as much as I can. "What's up?" I ask.

Looks like I'm not the only one having a meltdown—tears run down Olivia's face. Immediately, I put my hand on her shoulder and try to catch her eyes but she stares down at the phone in her hand.

"Olivia, it can't be that bad. Tell me what's wrong."

She snaps up, pressing her lips together, eyes wide going back and forth from me to the phone.

"You know how we spent an entire week filming, editing, loading, and getting social media posts ready for the entire duration of the lead up to the event? And we scheduled each post for a specific date and time, by channel?"

Of course I do. I'll never forget that week for as long as I live. The idea was good, in theory, but it was definitely an over commitment. But, Olivia and I worked together, far too many hours of overtime and take out Thai food, to get everything done.

"Yes," I answer, nervous for what's about to come next.

"Well, I don't know what happened, or how it happened, but all the posts just posted, to all channels. Every single piece of content in a single day." She shows me her phone, and I scroll the feed of our event account, which indeed has a flood of content.

Fuck me.

"We need to delete them but that means—"

"We'll lose all the edits," we say in tandem.

The freaking algorithm. All of the social media channels are at each other's throats, vying for everyone's attention and focus. If you don't edit your content, in that specific app for posting, it basically gets buried and no one will see it. Olivia and I decided we wouldn't use video or graphic design software, but that we'd edit each one in each app.

I put my head in my hands and then rub my temples. There's no amount of deep breathing or problem solving which will bring back the time and effort lost from this.

"There's nothing we can do besides delete it and redo the content for the next few days—get as far as you can with the rest of today. Can you do that?" I ask while my hand is on the door, eager to close it.

Olivia nods, pressing her phone to her chest.

I put on my fakest smile and nod my head up and down.

"Awesome. Let's meet tomorrow morning to figure out the rest," I say right before closing the door.

If there wasn't rice on the floor, I'd slide my back down the door and cry right here, but the thought of smashing rice into the carpet is too depressing, so I go to the side of my desk. I sit on the floor, lean back, and put my head in between my knees.

The tears are quick but the anxiety attack is quicker.

⌂ ⌂ ⌂ ⌂

I DIDN'T EVEN REALIZE my phone was dead. I plug it in, and as soon as it has enough juice, the notifications pour in: missed texts, calls, and a call from Holland.

I prop my phone up, using my laptop charging cord and a tape dispenser, and FaceTime Holland. Just when I think he's not going to pick up, his face fills the little screen. Simply seeing him lifts some of the heavy I went through today.

"Baby!" he says, his tone lifted and a smirk pulling at one side of his mouth.

"I'm sorry I missed your call earlier. Today's been... something." I finish typing out an email, click send, and shift my attention to my phone.

"Are you still at work?" Holland's face looks around, taking in the background which is obviously not my apartment.

"Yes, today was a disaster. I'm almost through my to-do list for the day and I'll be—"

He interrupts, "Did you eat? It's almost 9 PM."

Is it really? I knew it was late but didn't think it was *that* late.

My lack of answer gives me away.

"Ivy. You need to eat. You also need to go home. The work will be there tomorrow." The softness in his voice makes me ache for him, for my real home, his arms around me.

Naturally, I burst into tears. I launch into the long list of everything that went wrong today, leaving no detail spared. Holland listens to all of it, only interrupting to ask clarifying questions when the crying strangles my words.

When I'm done, Holland pauses, letting me wipe my eyes and try to gather myself.

"Wait a second, so a company sent you a rice sculpture, for a winter charity event? Rice, like the grain?" He laughs through the end of his question.

For the first time in a while, I let out an honest laugh. It's not one fueled by discomfort or sarcasm, but because something is funny.

"Yes! It makes no sense. You get it."

"I don't know about that, but I get you. I'm sorry today was hard. Tomorrow might be better... I'm betting there's going to be less rice, at least?" Holland shrugs his shoulders. He's sitting at the small table in the kitchen and seeing him in our space makes me feel better. "You're doing a good job, Ivy. Sparks is lucky to have you and this event is going to be amazing."

"I hope you're right." I dab the last of my tears.

"And don't ask yourself if you're giving enough. From here, it might be too much. Don't forget to take care of the woman I love so much." And if that wasn't sweet enough, Slate howls from somewhere. "Pretend Slate agrees and isn't being teased by a bird through the patio glassdoor." Holland laughs.

"I love you," I mutter as I slump back into the office chair, my stomach rumbling like my life is an ironic sitcom.

"Get out of the office, grab Thai food on your way home, and put Spider-Man on."

I put my elbows on my desk and set my head in my hands, grinning at Holland. I'm thinking back to when we first met and I asked if he was named after Tom Holland. Obviously he wasn't, considering he was born years before Tom Holland.

"I'm going to pack up and do just that. I'll text you when I'm home." Holland waves and ends the call.

I stare at the blank screen, thinking about how much my life has changed since I've met him. When this opportunity was offered to me, I was nervous to take it. I wondered how I'd feel coming back to the city

I left, the chaos and 24/7 vibes I once adored. Would I second-guess my decision to leave, moving to the Pacific Northwest, to the house tucked in the woods with the lodge owner?

The whole "city girl leaves her apartment for the man in the woods" line isn't lost on me. I know what it looks like from the outside, but, you know what? No one knows what that shift felt like—how I went from sprinting to a slow walk. My legs were about to give out from running, holding myself up through things I shouldn't have had to, and I needed a reset.

Holland, and the way he loves me, is the slow walk I didn't know I needed.

A smile, one I wasn't sure I'd find today, paints my lips as I pack my bag and leave the office.

CHAPTER FOUR
Holland

I HOLD THE SECRET in my fingers, turning it over and over. I finally built up enough courage, was going to come clean to Ivy, get this off my chest.

That didn't happen.

An empty rocks glass holds the remnants of my bourbon—the one I poured when I made the decision to tell Ivy what was going on. It's been too long keeping her in the dark. The wind whistles through the trees, pine branches move outside the floor to ceiling windows—probably my favorite part about this place. I can still hear my sister on the phone, telling me how she was arguing with the contractors on this type of window for the back wall.

In my hand is a check, made out to me, an offer to purchase The Emerald Canopy Lodge. Every time I look at the amount, I squint to make sure I'm getting all those zeroes right. There are oil smudges from the places my fingers have gripped and held it, over and over.

This all started with a guest, someone who stayed at the lodge, and ended with him stopping me at the lodge bar before he caught a flight.

"I know you don't know anything about me but I'm here to possibly make your life a thousand times easier. I work for an organization which focuses on merging sustainability forestation efforts and businesses like yours."

"If you have a sample for me, you can leave it at the front desk. I'll look when I have some time and we'll get back to you."

"No, it's nothing like that. This is a property I've had my eyes on for a while," the man looks around. He's tall, probably almost 6'6" and wearing jeans, black and white Nike sneakers, and a plain black hoodie. He senses me taking him in.

"Listen, it's a travel day," he gestures to his outfit, like I care if he's wearing a suit or not. "Holland, we purchase properties like yours, give it a burst in funding and help it thrive financially, while also maintaining and bettering the surrounding environment and ecosystems." He reaches into his pocket and pulls out a business card.

I grab it, too stunned to speak. The company, Greater When Green, itches my brain.

"Our CEO hosted a small retreat here a few years back. Since then, we've blown up and are really able to make a difference."

"I can't sell the lodge." I laugh as I look down at the card and back at him. This place was opened by my grandfather, run by my parents, and then my sister was supposed to take it over. Hazel never got the chance, so here I am, with the legacy business.

"It wouldn't be just selling. It'd be securing the lodge's legacy for many years past you and I. It's a bigger picture type of success."

My muscles are like stone, I'm not quite sure what to do. Part of me wonders if Ivy will hop out of a booth and scream "gotcha". This feels like a prank.

"The look you're giving me is normal. Listen, I know it's a lot without knowing much at all. My contact info is on the card. We'd love at least a meeting to talk about the offer. All I know is this place is too beautiful to not be around forever."

If there's something my grandfather instilled in me, it's that you always hear people out—that's what I did. Not right away, but after I'd been a moody bastard for far longer than anyone should've accepted, I knew I needed to at least hear them out.

Greater When Green was surprisingly good—the associates like-able—with many success stories with organizations which have taken them up on their offers.

The things they wanted to do at the lodge, add on, enhance, would bring more revenue long term, and make it even more stable. It's not like we're hurting for money but there's not a strong strategy behind that. It's mostly that I haven't done something crippling and terribly wrong, on accident, up to this point.

The offer I hold in my hand, allows me to keep working at the lodge, along with the entire current staff, but giving up ownership and big picture decisions. The official line is I'd still be involved in those conversations, but it's hard to tell if that's accurate. I'd have to see it to believe it.

The cabin Hazel built would become mine, along with the property it sits on, as well as some surrounding—a solid bonus with the offer. Calling it a cabin still feels ridiculous, since it's nicer than most homes, but that's what it's technically referred to.

Hazel. My heart aches over my sister. It's been years since she died, but there are times, like right now, where I'd give damn near anything to talk to her. The lodge was always Hazel's happy place. Her safe place. Am I betraying her memory by selling it? Or am I honoring her by making it more stable? Everything is jumbled in my brain and it fucking hurts—like when you keep biting the spot on your lip, over and over again.

If I would've gotten this offer when Hazel died, I would've taken it without question. Something like this would've been my saving grace. I haven't talked to my parents about the pending offer, but I know what they will say: this is your decision and we support you either way. The same way they tried to jump in when I was practically killing myself taking everything over after Hazel.

With the compensation, I could still work, if I wanted to, but I wouldn't need to. Or, Ivy could quit her job and do something else? The point is that the money is substantial.

It might take the pressure off. I could work at the lodge but not be responsible for its success after that point. I've poured myself into this place for years and I've taken care of it, but how long do I want to do that for?

That's the question my therapist asked when we talked about the potential offer.

I still don't have an answer.

I do know that I can't keep this from Ivy much longer. While the lodge is my family legacy, she's part of my family, and I could never make this decision without her.

At first, I thought the whole Greater When Green thing was bullshit; that there'd be nothing to share about the odd encounter with the man when I was in the bar. With each meeting, email, further discussion, I then didn't know how to bring it up.

That's what tonight was for, but she was spiraling. I know she can take care of herself, but I remember what she was like when we first met: striving for perfection, no matter how much of herself it took.

I know this event it's important, but Ivy keeping herself whole is a non-negotiable.

Grabbing my phone from the table, I text Vivian.

At least being back in New York means Ivy has Vivian. If I'm not able to be there to support Ivy, she's the next person I'd pick. Hell, she might be my first pick, depending on the situation.

Note to self: stay in Vivian's good graces. That woman terrifies me. Even from the first time I met her, a quick trip to the lodge when Ivy got stuck here. She has a way of talking that makes you want to sit straight and listen but she's also capable of being the life of the party.

Slate cries by the door, pawing at his leash. He's never been shy about what he wants. I wish I was more like Slate in that way.

CHAPTER FIVE
Ivy

11 DAYS UNTIL RED CARPET EVENT

Snow blankets the sidewalks and streets as the sun peeks over the skyline. I step out from the warmth of my apartment building, and inhale a slow, long breath—letting the chill of the morning invade my lungs. I tilt my face to the sky; fat flakes showing no sign of stopping, as they pepper my nose and cheeks.

I'm still not one to load up on outdoor activities but I've always loved the snow. Winters in New York are different than out west. Some people might wake up and see snow and think it's another thing they have to deal with, but it's something that immediately lifts my mood.

"What the fuck are you doing?" Vivian interrupts my snowy moment of gratitude. "I told you I'd come up since it's freezing out here." She shivers.

"You didn't need to! I love this weather." I wrap her up in a hug.

She tolerates me for a few seconds. "Less standing, more walking to yoga." She's already two steps ahead of me, eager to get out of the chilled air.

Yoga is only four blocks from my place and I swear Viv would take a cab if I didn't beg her to walk.

"Give me the rundown on the event. How are we doing?" She tightens the checkered scarf around her neck, her short blonde hair pulled back in the cutest ponytail. Viv changes her hair, cut and color, like it's nothing. Of course she can pull everything off, from the long jet black layers to a red pixie cut she had a few years back.

Viv is such a trooper. She's heard me talk about this thing up and down for months now. She knows it, inside and out, and is a great sounding board when I'm stuck. I go through all the solutions I found in the last two days. We're still loading in content, and not trusting a scheduler, but everything else seems like it's back to where it should be, or there's at least a back up plan.

"Ah! Also approved the ice sculpture and you'll be happy to know it's starch free." I bump my winter coat padded shoulder into Viv's.

The rice sculpture has turned into an inside joke, one I don't think I'll ever get over.

"Amazing. Did you work already this morning?" She asks a question that she knows the answer to.

"Only a couple hours." I answer like we're not cautiously walking snowy sidewalks at 7:30 AM for a Saturday yoga class.

"Ivy. You need more sleep and regular meals. Let's do better this week, yeah?"

I know Holland keeps in touch with Viv, which means they probably compare notes about my bad days. At first, it made me feel like I didn't know how to take care of myself but I'm lucky to have people who love me like they do. They mean well.

"Okay, Holland, I'll do that." I say it with a wink so she knows I'm joking. Well, sort of.

We reach the yoga studio, Viv runs to pull the door open, slipping a little before steadying herself with the handle. Her eyes are so wide they could fall right out of her head.

"I would've laughed so hard if you fell, after I figured out you were okay." I put my gloved hands on the side of my face and giggle, my brain playing the scenario out the other way.

"You're the one who makes me walk," Vivian whines. "Get your ass inside." She pulls the door open for me.

— ⟁ ⟁ ⟁ ⟁ —

No matter how many yoga classes I go to, I swear they are equally hard. It's like I can't get my mind and body to cooperate. The days my muscles are long and pliable are the days my brain is running its own marathon, or vice versa.

This morning, both parts were difficult. I've spent most of my week huddled over my laptop, tensing my shoulders, and clenching my jaw—it's not surprising that stretching and lengthening wasn't easy. My brain kept thinking of all the things I needed to accomplish, which to be fair, is better than the mantra of "fuck, this is so hard."

I'll take what I can get.

"The best part of yoga is the coffee and treats after," Viv says, while holding a steaming mug of black coffee. She's dramatic and still wearing her scarf, claiming she's still cold.

We're at one of our favorite coffee shops, just a block from yoga. There's no way I could've convinced Viv to walk any further than that.

"I don't disagree," I take a drink of my cinnamon latte; the warmth of the coffee plus the pleasant spice of the cinnamon is perfect for a winter morning.

"Are you excited to go home for a quick visit before the event?" Viv asks, while ripping part of a cinnamon roll from our shared pastry plate and putting it in her mouth. "I'm sure Holland will be extra grumpy for you."

I roll my eyes at Viv before answering. "A thousand times yes. I can obviously take my laptop, and wrap up whatever is going on here, but—"

She leans over and puts my face in her hands, and thankfully she just wiped the cinnamon roll crumbs off her fingers. "Listen to me. You're going home, to your man, to have wild and hot I-missed-you-sex. I don't want to hear about your fucking laptop." She lightly shakes my head for emphasis.

I smile, bunching my cheeks and she lets me go.

"I'm serious! This is the old you. I thought workaholic Ivy was dead and buried. Did we resurrect her and I missed it? I thought I was clear—I want to join any and all resurrections." She points her finger at me, giving me a proper scolding.

"She *is* dead, but this event means a lot to me. It's a solid opportunity with an even better cause. I just want to do a good job." I've never been able to explain this well. It's like I know some of these habits aren't healthy but I'd take that over falling even an inch short.

"No, you're trying to be superhuman. The cause might be great, but your mental health is not something you should sacrifice. I'm just saying, enjoy the visit. You need a break." She lifts her hands up like she's waving the white flag.

"I will. This is the longest we've been apart, except for when I left the very first time." I cross my arms, daydreaming of our teary goodbye in the airport. Someone offered to take our photo, Slate included, and it's one I have framed at our place at the lodge.

Viv sighs out a breath, looking around the room, dramatically, before she lands her eyes on mine. "You know, when you told me you were moving out of the city, I barely believed you. For someone who has been an indoor cat most of her life, gotta say, the lodge life looks good on you."

I grin at my best friend, one of the souls closest to mine. "I know. Life's so unpredictable sometimes."

She's not wrong and this is a thought I've had myself. If you would've told me that I'd end up falling in love, on a work trip, in a place where there are mountains and trees but no Uber, or a Target, I would've never believed you.

"I mean, you used to listen to stock sounds of traffic, like city white noise to fall asleep. Do you ever still do that?" Her brows raise with her question.

"Sometimes. Mostly when I'm missing you." I wink at her and she shimmies her shoulders in response. "I sleep a lot better when I'm with Holland and Slate. I still do my deep breathing and stretching routine before bed, but it mostly settles me. Before, it felt like I was grasping at anything that could help me sleep."

I'm still an anxious millenial but my sleep has drastically improved in the last year. Maybe Jack, the horrible ex, was so toxic that his vibes actually were ruining my sleep schedule. Probably not, but every once in a while Jack deserves a mental dig—even if I'm the only one who can hear it.

"Anything I can help with while you're gone? I know it's just a few days," Vivian offers.

"Actually, would you mind doing a drink tasting?" It's barely a favor because I know how this is right up her alley.

"Say less. Where should I go?" I write down the name of the bar that's going to do the drink catering for the event and her eyes light up.

"This place is on my list! Absolutely."

"They make their own spirits and are just starting out. If the drinks are as good as I think they're going to be, it's a perfect fit. You know the drill; save your receipt and Sparks will reimburse you."

"Thank you for trusting me with the highest of honors." Viv playfully puts her hands on her chest and raises the other in the air.

It's a small thing but I'm so thankful for her. Honestly, I'm decisioned out. I don't want to pick between another thing at this moment. There's no more mental space available.

A savory croissant stares at me from our plate, so I rip it in half and let the buttery pastry melt in my mouth. It's filled with bacon and Gruyère cheese, and it's one of the best croissants I've tasted. I let out a moan which has Viv reaching for the other half before I get greedy and eat the entire thing.

"Do you really not know who will be walking the red carpet at the gala?" She gives me a side stare, one I've seen more than once—it's the one she uses to try and get me to tell her something—like she ever needs to try *that* hard.

"I really don't," I say, taking a drink of coffee after. "Stella is in charge of the guest list and I'm thankful."

With Viv's question, I'm back to the gala. Nervous energy jumpstarts my thoughts, my worries. I want to do anything in my power to make this a success—it's important to me for so many different reasons. I know that I'm only one person, a small piece of the puzzle, but it's not above me to try and do the whole damn puzzle myself.

I try to quiet my brain, still filling my thoughts with all that's left to do. I try to quiet the neverending to-do list but I'm unsuccessful. Being mindful is something I've worked on for what feels like my entire life. When I can be mindful in situations, both socially and with food, I'm a happier version of myself.

Unfortunately, my busy brain wins and I lean into the chaos.

CHAPTER SIX
Ivy

"How does this typo happen? Seriously? I need an explanation." Stella says, showing me a few print materials that are clearly incorrect—one is simply the wrong size but the other has the word "galla" instead of "gala".

My stomach flips. We're basically a week away and things that should be drop dead easy are nothing but problems. "Maybe I shouldn't leave?" I ask as I flip through a botched order of print materials, the latest on a long list of mistakes. If there was a leaderboard, the rice sculpture is at the top, claiming the spot of most ridiculous and most disappointing of the mistakes.

"That isn't even an option," Stella replies, putting her hand flat on the page I was looking at, capturing my full attention. "We'll be fine here. I'll get this monstrosity fixed and then we'll be almost back on track." She grabs the stack of papers, pulling them to her and out of my reach.

"Are you sure?" My stomach drops thinking of leaving so close to the thing I've been planning for months, especially when it seems like anything that could go wrong, would. It's kind of selfish to leave at this juncture, honestly.

"A thousand percent. I'm also fluent in Ivy and I know you're convincing yourself that you need to stay and it's not true. Your brain is telling you lies."

Damn, she's good. I also feel like I may have divulged a little too much when it comes to "how is therapy going" because that's a line straight from my therapist.

Stella smiles, making eye contact. "The plane tickets are paid for. You fly out the day after tomorrow and it's only for a few days. We'll see you next week. Remember, we even have an extra travel day accounted for, so you should be back the day before the event." She puts her hands on my shoulders. "Plenty of time." She gives me a little shake.

"But, all of these things keep coming up and who knows what else will?" I plead.

"You've done your part, Ivy. And it doesn't matter whether you're here or at home, whatever's going to come up will *still* come up," she says, organizing the print materials on the desk. "We can only do so much. Plus, what fun would this be if it was easy as pie?"

She's right. I'll obviously have my laptop and will be able to assist with whatever I can. We're in the stage of deliveries and preparations at the venue; it shouldn't matter that I'll be working remote.

"I'll make sure to stay on top of my email and you can call if you need anything," I say, trying to sound helpful, but mostly I think I'm trying to convince myself.

"I know you will but try to enjoy the time. You've been away from home for a few weeks. Do some recharging before the gala." Stella tucks a piece of her chic, gray bob haircut behind her ears.

I want to ask if she's positively sure. As the battle of reassurance and being a burden declares a winner, I say nothing. I reach for a hug and smile as she pats my back.

Many people don't hug their boss but they don't have a Stella.

Fine, I'll go home. I'll take the gracious gift of time, from my work-life-balancing boss, and enjoy myself. That doesn't mean I can't try and fit in as much work in before I get on that plane.

I walk to Olivia's cubicle, finding the intern dressed in a dark navy blazer with her hair pulled back in a sleek bun, and knock on one of the standing walls. When she turns and sees me, she smiles, something we've been working on. I don't see any tears or a wobbly lip in sight.

"I have a proposition for you. Why don't we work late tonight, dinner on Sparks, and you can take the day off when I fly out?" I want to be productive but I still don't need to instill bad habits into the fresh intern.

She smiles, nods yes, and hands me a stack of takeout menus from a desk drawe. Three of the five are for Thai restaurants—my favorite.

I feel like Olivia and I could be friends after this.

CHAPTER SEVEN
Holland

Slate hangs his head out the truck window, cracked enough for him to put his paws and head outside but not enough for him to jump out—that's a lesson I learned the hard way.

We're parked outside of arrivals, waiting for Ivy to walk out those glass doors. She texted about twenty minutes ago, saying she was waiting for her luggage.

I can't wait to see my girl. It's like Slate knows we're waiting for her because he's howling, in public, causing quite the scene—not the first time and won't be the last.

Between keeping the offer a secret and my routine being turned upside down with Ivy traveling for work, it's like my bones don't fit my skin. I told my therapist and she again reminded me of the anxiety and how keeping secrets is not in my best interest.

Believe me, I know.

Ever since I told Ivy about Hazel, the terrible trip home where I heard the news that would change my life forever, in detail, it's like a small door has opened, and I find myself sharing more. It might just be with Ivy, sometimes Bea, but each time makes me feel a little lighter—a little more like I can comfortably fit in my bones.

Slate tries to jump out the window and I know that he sees her. I hurry to the passenger side, before Slate chokes himself, open the door, grabbing the leash at the last moment.

She kneels down, on the questionable sidewalk, and let's Slate run into her arms. People walking past her are looking at us with a mix of what the hell and how cute. I've got one foot in each camp.

"Slaaaaate," Ivy croons and hearing her voice is like a cozy blanket—one that brings relief from a constant chattering of your teeth.

I take in the moment; it may not be soothing, like Hazel always taught me, but it's one I want to remember. The sound of travel and traffic are in the background but seeing Ivy and Slate together like this, squeezes my heart.

I feel like when you date someone, there's supposed to be those moments of doubts, questions you may or may not be able to answer. Truthfully, once she found her way into my soul, closed off and ice cold on its best day, it was over.

There's no one else for me. And I fucking love it.

When she stands up, her green eyes are filled with tears, because she wouldn't be my Ivy if it wasn't a tearful hello.

Instead of saying anything, I reach for her hand and pull her close to me. Her lower lip shakes as she tries to smile and I put an end to that by putting my mouth on hers.

Her lips, soft as ever, feel like home. The grin taking over my lips is inevitable, and she laughs as I smile into our kiss. She wraps her arms around my neck, pushing her hips closer to me—Slate jumps up and down, getting both of our thighs.

I almost forget we're in public until I hear someone whistle as they walk by. We're those people. Never in a million years did I think I'd be someone who elicits that kind of reaction outside an airport—both with Ivy and the stranger passing by.

"I missed you," she says, looking up at me.

"I'm glad you're home," I reply, kissing her forehead and wrapping her up.

— ⌂ ⌂ ⌂ ⌂ —

SLATE, EXHAUSTED FROM THE overstimulation and car ride, sprints into the house as soon as I take his harness off. He finds his bed, does some lazy circles, and plops down.

"The hardest life," Ivy jokes as we step inside. "I'm going to put all of this away."

Not surprising—she's the quickest unpacker I think I've ever met. Ivy takes her bag and heads for our room. I sit at the small table in our kitchen, thinking about the folded up check and offer sheet tucked away in a drawer. Having her and this piece of paper in the same place makes my skin hot.

I can't do this another minute. I have to tell her—come clean.

As soon as I make the decision, her voice cuts through my guilt trip. "Holland, why are you still downstairs?" she asks, her voice suggestive.

Fuck.

Taking the stairs, two at a time, I walk into our room to find Ivy wearing lingerie, kneeling on the bed, with her legs tucked under her ass. The emerald lace is a contrast to her milky skin and almost a perfect match to her eyes—the ones I could get lost in.

She stands on her knees and does a come closer gesture with her finger, the other hand propped on her hip. My dick twitches in my joggers.

I close the space between us and immediately take both hands, weaving them through her hair, the nape of her neck, and pull her lips to mine. Her mouth parts, letting my tongue graze hers. Ivy bites my lower lip, setting the tone.

The groan I let out is unplanned and the most visceral of reactions.

"Did you miss me?" she teases.

My response is a series of quick kisses and nips from her jawline down to her neck. I take my time as she lets out these little laughs and moans.

"I could live off those sounds," I say before peppering a line of kisses on her collarbone.

The emerald lace is bunched at the top of the bra, letting the fabric lightly touch the tops of her breasts. After a playful hair pull, my fingers walk a line from the nape of her neck to the heavenly spot where the lace meets skin.

"New York isn't all bad. It has things like this for me to bring home," Ivy laughs as I take her in.

I put my face between her breasts and she leans back, giving me a bit more access. I take my tongue from the top of her cleavage over to one of her perfect tits.

I catch her eyes and kneel on the bed with her, needing to be closer.

"Were you thinking of me when you bought this?" I kiss the bulge of her breasts, almost spilling over the lingerie top—the curves I've desperately missed.

"Only ever you, Holland." She yips as I pull the fabric down, enough to put a nipple in my mouth. Flicking it with my tongue, I take in as much of her as I can. "I was especially thinking of how you'd need to be gentle with these panties. No ripping."

Her telling me what to do makes me want to scream. I put my hands under her armpits, her arms wrapping around my neck, as I pick her up, off her knees.

She wraps her legs around my hips, while I'm still kneeling. My hands move to her back, unclasping her bra. No ripping...

When her tits spill out, I lightly push her on her back. The friction of her rubbing on my pants, my dick hard, is heaven and hell. The pleasure of any touch, feeling, the one I've missed but am aching for more.

She extends her legs and all I can stare at are those delicate fucking panties. I hook a finger on the band and pull them down just a little. I kiss the sensitive spot underneath her belly button before hitching a leg up and kissing up and down her inner thigh.

Those thighs. Fuck, I've missed them.

I lightly bite when I get close to the edge of her panties and Ivy squirms beneath me. My girl loves being teased. I lightly lick up and down before placing the softest of kisses, while my other hand grips her ass.

"I need, fuck. I need more," Ivy says, voice hoarse and breathless as she bows off the bed.

"What do you need more of?" I love making her tell me exactly what to do.

She moans as I pull her panties down an inch further, kissing closer to her center.

"You know what I need." Her words are quick as I lick closer and closer to where she needs but I won't go there until she says it. "I need you to make me come."

I grin as I move kisses to the top of where the fabric meets her skin. "How do you want to come, baby?"

"Use your mouth and your fingers," she says as she moves underneath me, trying to find the pressure and pace that works best for her.

When I feel her eyes on me, I tilt my face up to see her watching me. Fuck, why is this so hot? I give her a devilish grin before torturing her with the slowest pull of her panties, all the way down.

"You told me to be gentle."

Ivy puts her hands in my hair, still writhing her hips, and presses enough for me to know she's trying to be in control. So, I let her.

I kiss her clit and am rewarded with a sweet, sweet whimper.

CHAPTER EIGHT
Ivy

6 DAYS UNTIL RED CARPET EVENT

Holland finally puts his mouth where it belongs. My hands grab onto his hair, moving his head and mouth to get the angle and pressure I need.

He slips a finger in and growls, "Is all this for me? You're so wet."

I whine at the pressure and his mouth missing from my center. "It's been a while." I struggle to get the words out. My heart feels like it could beat right out of my chest.

Holland is like a man possessed. His mouth, fingers, and hands are everywhere, inching me closer and closer. I look down to see his dark hair sticking through my fingers; lifting my shoulder changes how his mouth is hitting my clit.

He speeds up before going torturously slow—my hips writhe for more.

"I'm so close," I try to say, but words, and breaths, are hard to find. My climax builds, the itch in my low belly almost scratched.

He uses another finger, moans into my clit, and I'm a goner. My orgasm hits me so hard I can't help but scream. Holland rides it out with me, his hands and mouth still going, as I move and wriggle my hips and body beneath him. He uses one hand to put pressure on my lower stomach, pinning me in place but also making my finish even stronger.

My body twitches and trembles as I try to catch my breath. I look to see Holland watching me, wearing a devilish grin pulled up on one side, his lips wet with me.

"Okay, that was... that was..." I rake my hands up my body, grabbing my breasts, up my neck, and into my own hair, as I catch my breath.

"What word are you looking for?" he teases me.

"I can't even tell you. My brain... needs a second."

At that moment, Holland pushes himself off the bed, standing. All I can focus on is his erection straining his pants.

"Your turn," I say, looking from his eyes, to his dick, and back again.

"How do you want me?" Holland asks, reaching for his shirt and pulling it up and over his head. His dark locks are a mess from my grabby fingers and his cheeks are flushed pink.

Holland is a runner; I shouldn't be surprised when I see him without a shirt on, but it doesn't get old. I take in his strong shoulders, broad chest, and each of his abs, lightly flexing with his quick breath.

"Take your pants off and lay on the bed," I instruct as I take my panties all the way off.

I watch as Holland takes off his pants, and briefs, and my mouth is watering. I've never wanted someone the way I want him. When he lays back, he puts his hands behind his head, propped up on the pillows. His muscles bulge in his arms in this position—his 'H' tattoo on full display.

I straddle him, putting my body over his, and take my hands from his shoulders down his frame. I touch his pecs, his abs, and end at the top of his thighs.

When I wrap my hand around his cock, I feel precum on the tip. I love how his body reacts to making me finish.

I move my hand up, touch the head, and back down the shaft.

"Easy... it's been a while, remember?" Holland teases, catching my eyes.

I remove my hands, but place a soft kiss at the tip of his cock.

"You're killing me," Holland groans, shifting his hips, and it makes me feel like a queen. I love being able to get him to react this way.

I lift myself up and then slowly lower myself on his dick. The fullness is something I've missed and to be honest, I'm not sure I'll ever be used to it. Holland grabs my hips, fingers digging into my skin. I toss my long brunette hair over my shoulder before I lower myself and put my lips on Hollands.

The way his mouth presses into mine is like we were meant to be together. Lock and key. Puzzle pieces. I'll never get tired of kissing this man.

Holland's hands, firm and strong, reach from my hips to my lower back. He pulls me to him, setting the pace. I rock forward, pushing my hips and pulling my hands up my body until I reach my hair. I wrap my fingers around strands of hair and lightly tug.

"I love when you do that," Holland says. "You're fucking incredible." His voice is gravel and his eyes are devious, golden pools. I'm ready for him to pull me under.

My soul shines at the praise.

Holland places the pad of his thumb on my bundle of nerves, a game changer. I move, almost frantically, over him. Running. Chasing. Wanting more.

"I love when *you* do *that*." My voice is breathless and quick. I place my hands on Holland's chest, feeling the muscles underneath.

"So good," I moan out, relishing the slight change in position, my orgasm closer than ever.

I roll my hips, what I need just in reach.

"Come for me, Ivy," Holland says and it's all I need. I move my hips faster, the sound of my breath is no match for the beating of my heart. He doesn't stop touching my clit and I come while I ride him.

"Fuck," he says as he comes along side me. I love hearing him like this, all out of breath, and full of need.

I clench and shiver around him but my body can't stop moving. We ride out the end of our climaxes together and I collapse onto his chest. It's like there's a string between us and someone pulls it tight.

"Welcome home." Holland wraps his arm around me and kisses the top of my head.

CHAPTER NINE
Holland

I DIDN'T EXPECT IVY to like the rainy season, but she loves to surprise me. November in the Pacific Northwest means you can almost always bet on rain and my girl doesn't bat an eye, as long as she's prepared.

"Come on, Slate. Let me zip you up," she says while corralling the most spoiled dog in the universe into his raincoat. Slate loves it because it means he gets to go outside on a day he'd typically only be allowed to stare out the window.

Ivy stands, clipping Slate's leash to the back of the coat, and the smile she wears stops me. My city girl, who didn't bring any shoes other than high heels on her first trip, is beaming over a rainy day. Or maybe it's seeing Slate in clothes?

Pulling out her phone, she opens her weather app for what I'm guessing is the ninth time since we woke up. Ivy may have acclimated to the outdoors a bit but her need to be prepared, planning for any and all scenarios, hasn't shifted. I wouldn't want her any other way.

"We should be good for a forty-minute walk before the rain picks up," she says while putting her phone back in her pocket. The hood from Ivy's black jacket is pulled up so she lifts her chin up a little more to catch my eyes—fucking gorgeous.

When she opens the door, Slate's leash in her hand, I can't help but laugh at her when Slate pulls and she almost slips in her blush pink boots.

Rain falls onto leaves littering the ground, the pitter patter scratches part of my brain just right. The three of us walk in slow, comfortable silence. If we go too fast, the serenity of the walk will be lost to Slate's panting and gremlin breathing.

I reach for her free hand and intermingle my gloved fingers with hers. Ivy looks over at me, her eyes like the early sign of spring, green and vibrant. Her cheeks, damp with the rain and pink with cold, bunch as she smiles at me.

My stomach drops and I have to catch my breath. I don't know if that "is this for real" feeling will ever stop. I hope it doesn't.

We reach our halfway mark, a look out point, which shows the mountains and trees for miles and miles. It's like you can see so far into the world. This is one of our favorite places to come and watch the sunset but today it's nothing but fluffy, gray clouds, heavy with rain.

"Come here, good boy," I call as I kneel to pick up Slate and hold him to me. I know it makes Ivy nervous to have him on the leash as we get closer to the edge.

Slate rests his head on my shoulder as I hold him to my chest. Ivy steps closer, wrapping her arm around my back and leaning her head on me. Even in the rain, I can make out her smell of lavender.

I close my eyes and breathe in, nice and slow. Rain hits the branches and the pine trees holding onto their needles. Even though it's a gloomy sort of day, I can still see the light behind the clouds, the sun trying its best. Slate's heartbeat is quick and I feel his breaths, in and out, as I hold him.

A soothing moment. Just like my sister, Hazel, taught me. I feel Ivy doing the same thing. I catalog this moment between the three of us and file it away in the place I keep many others like it.

"I love the rain," Ivy's voice is quiet.

"I know you do." I look at her before placing a soft kiss on her mouth. She tastes like coffee and sugar.

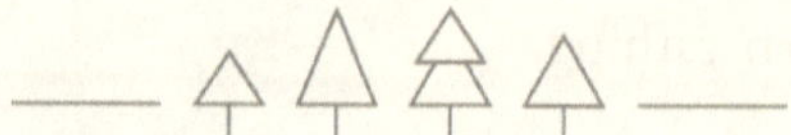

AFTER CLEANING SLATE UP and leaving him with a blanket straight from the dryer, Ivy and I head to the lodge.

We walk into the front doors and here a squeal before we're three steps in. Bea runs over, bells from her headband literally jingling, from the front desk and wraps Ivy in a hug, before putting a loud kiss on her wet cheek before shaking Ivy back and forth.

If you made Bea pick between myself, Ivy, and Slate, I'm a little afraid I might come in last. Wouldn't have it any other way though. It's nice seeing how Ivy fits in my life.

"It's so good to see you! You must be freezing. Let's get you some hot chocolate and lunch." She talks so quick there isn't time for Ivy to say anything. Bea puts a hand around Ivy's arm and starts walking towards the restaurant.

"Hey, Bea," I say with sarcasm and follow behind.

"Quit with that, Holland. I see you all the time," she lovingly snaps over her shoulder. Ivy laughs and it echoes in the lobby.

"Any fun stories about the city? How is Vivian? Is she dating anyone? We've been texting, did she tell you?" Ivy watches Bea with love in her eyes.

We slide into a booth, Ivy and Bea sitting next to each other, and me across. Without being asked, the bartender sees Ivy and immediately brings over a mug of fresh hot chocolate with a small dish with anything and everything you may want to add to your cup: marshmallows, sprinkles, peppermint sticks, butterscotch chips, a ramekin full of caramel, and another full of whipped cream.

Everyone knows Ivy is a sugar fiend. She's also the reason we put the hot chocolate on the restaurant menu, and added the mini bar for guests to add whatever they'd like. Ivy tested it out one day while I was running an event and she was working on some stuff for Sparks in the restaurant. Not only do guests love it, but it's one of the things they post most about reviews when they stay at the lodge, or at least that's what Ivy tells me. I stay off the internet as much as possible.

After we place our lunch orders, Bea says, "Tell me everything about the event."

Ivy's shoulders immediately slump, as she rolls her head side to side, stretching her neck. "It's been a mess." The light falls from her face. "No matter what, anything that can go wrong has. I feel like I may not be the person for this thing." Her voice dwindles almost to a whisper as the sentence trails. She seems to slump further into the booth.

This reminds me so much of our first night here—how she reacted when that drunk idiot Royce Jones came in, making her uncomfortable. My blood pumps thinking about how what he did later was much worse, forcing himself on Ivy, while I was in the other room.

It also reminds me how Bea has the knack for getting someone to talk about anything. She's been at the lodge, and damn near part of my family, for twenty-seven years—we just celebrated her anniversary last week.

Between hot chocolate refills, Ivy launches into the saga which is a long list of unfortunate events and mishaps—everything from rice sculptures, invitation delays, and people backing out of committed work. She does this thing where she rolls her eyes and makes an excuse for someone else, claiming responsibility, when it's nowhere near her fault.

My heart stings while I take in this version of Ivy. The one I haven't seen in a minute—shrinking, doubtful, and ridiculously hard on herself. My own shoulders slump as I think about the secret I'm keeping, how I need to tell Ivy. How I need her to help me make this decision.

She's got so much going on, I don't want to pile on more to my girl who is already struggling to stand. Maybe I wait until the event is over? We can talk about it when she's home, for good. That seems like the best course of action.

I hope.

CHAPTER TEN
Ivy

4 DAYS UNTIL RED CARPET EVENT

I'm walking the red carpet, my hair slinking down my shoulder, pulled to one side with a jeweled barrette. It's finally here and I feel like I can breathe a little. The paparazzi is out, just like we'd hoped, as people start to arrive.

I go to take a step, but my shoes aren't quite right, as the back slips off my heel—they might be a half size too big. How did I miss that? The toes of my high heels keep kicking the front of my dress, which now seems like it's a bit too long. I roll out my shoulders, making sure the top of my dress isn't caught on something—making sure it's on right.

My hands go to brush the front of the dress and the crimson red polish is chipped on one finger. How in the world? I just got this gel manicure yesterday; there's no way it's already chipping. While I look closer at the nail in question, little fucking traitor, I almost trip because my dress really is too long.

The sounds of clicking cameras are loud in my ears, followed by laughs and snickers from others on the carpet. My almost fall didn't go unnoticed. I take in a deep breath, trying to soothe my racing heart, but instead, I choke on air. I try to cover my mouth as fast as I can but the cough is offensively loud and if people missed my earlier discretion, they *definitely* heard this.

I try to focus on something at the end of the walk. My brain needs a focal point before I lose any of the remaining composure I have left. Someone turns around, tall and wearing a designer suit, and it's like he moves in slow motion. When he sees me, his mouth creeps up into a grin which is too wide for his face.

Royce.

I gasp and feel the color leave my face.

When Royce takes a quick step towards me, I lean back and almost stumble. I go to turn and walk back to where I came from, anywhere but here. I can't be here with him. He's supposed to be in jail. This time, my heels get caught in my dress and I do fall on my hands and knees.

As I'm trying to catch my breath, a hand grips my upper arm—trying to pick me up.

And then my eyes snap open.

"Ivy," Holland says, words deliberate and firm. "You're having a nightmare… I think." He moves hair from my forehead, his thumb ending up on my jaw, slowly moving back and forth. I lean into his touch, closing my eyes. The blood pounds through my anxious veins.

It was all a dream. I let out a slow breath and let my head fall back on my pillow. "What time is it?" I ask, after I've gotten myself together enough to form a coherent sentence. Holland's golden eyes, like honey, ground me even further.

"It's 6 AM. I'm going to the lodge–I know you wanted to work this morning. This place is all yours." He kisses my forehead. "There's breakfast downstairs and butterscotch cake on the counter. Don't be afraid to eat real food before the sugar." Holland shakes his head but he's the one who helps feed this sugar addiction.

"You're too good to me."

"When you're ready for lunch, come by the lodge," Holland suggests as he stands from the bed. He's wearing dark denim jeans and a light blue long sleeve, the one that's soft and has the waffle texture I like so much.

As Holland pads down the stairs, Slate steals the empty spot of the bed. He nudges my hand, looking for attention, before he plops down, his back to my front—he loves being the little spoon. There's no way I can get out of bed now, so I set an alarm.

Slate falls asleep quickly; his breathing sets a soothing pace. I embrace the big spoon position and soak in the extra hour of sleep.

THE KITCHEN BAR SERVES as my makeshift office today. While there's quite a few places I can work, I typically gravitate to the kitchen. The timer beeps—time for coffee—and I plunge down the French press. I pour a cup, only adding a single sugar today. Holland is a bit of a coffee snob—we always have the best freshly ground beans.

I wrap my fingers around the mug and move in front of the floor to ceiling windows that serve as the kitchen wall. This view still surprises me, the way it did the first time I saw it. It always makes me feel so small and there's so much to conquer. Try. Do.

Sipping the coffee, rich with notes of chocolate and hazelnuts, I breathe in deep, sinking into the slow exhale. Heavy rain drops hit and pepper the windows. Cooler than yesterday, an ice watch shows on my weather app whenever I open it. There's a storm system coming, making the November weather much cooler than we're used to.

Yesterday was a disconnect day; I didn't check my email or do anything work related. Since I work a more flexible schedule, and am after an optimal work-life balance, I try to mark blocks like this on my calendar. Boundaries are important but that doesn't mean they're easy to follow, even when I set them for myself.

I used to think if I worked constantly, always brought my A-game, being prepared for anything, I'd be ready for anything. But real life doesn't work like that. No matter how much you prepare, something—completely out of your control—can spiral, taking you out in the process. Work is only a piece of my life and it doesn't get the privilege of owning all of me.

Oh, therapy. How you've opened my eyes.

I open my laptop, eager to get into my email. I have my notebook handy, ready to make a list of tasks. Is there anything better than making, and crossing things off, a to-do list?

317 unread emails.

After getting through the first fifty emails, things are kind of a mixed bag. Yes, we got the print materials corrected and they look great, but there seems to be something that isn't quite right to balance out every win, like the shipping delay for the Delatou wines. It's no one's "fault" exactly, just a case of a missing box or two. Don't we *all* know about that. My shoulders are up near my ears and my fingers stab my laptop keys harder than necessary. I go to lick my lips but they're pressed hard into each other.

The list I'm currently working on is titled "Day of To-Do's". Things like picking up—and individually packing—cookies, waiting for the custom drink stirrers to be delivered and get to the bar staff, and finalizing packing the SWAG bags for attendees.

Almost everything on this list is a finishing touch, which I'd argue is one of the most important. People are constantly invited to dinners, for this charity or that, and it's hard to stand out. Yes, I want to raise a ton of money for Ours and Yours and Chin Up, but I want people to feel like they got their money's worth, and most of all, had a great time.

I didn't make a single decision based on budget or something "seeming good enough." If it isn't something I'd be impressed—or satisfied with—it's not happening at this event. This is also the first time Sparks Wellness is dipping their toe into this type of venture—some say you live and die by the first impression.

The goal is to always have everything taken care of, before the actual day or start time of the event, but you don't win them all. We're working with quite a few vendors and many of them seem to have their own challenges.

It's official: I'll basically have a full day of work prior to the actual event. Luckily, my black Chanel dress, which isn't too long, is hanging on a velvet hanger in my New York apartment. I have everything I need to get myself ready and I'm thankful none of that has gone wrong.

I'm putting my tenth task on my 'Day of to-do' list when my pen runs out. There isn't much else I'm more particular about than my writing utensil. Being left-handed means finding things that don't smear when you write and typically missing out on the glitter gel pen craze in high school.

My laptop bag doesn't have any extras—I make a mental note to change that—but I know there are some spares in the kitchen. I open a drawer and see one before it rolls to the back. Holland isn't one for clutter, so it's common for drawers to be almost empty. I put my hand in the back, feeling for it so I can get back to my list. When I grab the pen, and what feels like a piece of paper, I pull my hand out.

It's actually three pieces of paper, folded, and the header makes me freeze.

Formal Offer to Purchase The Emerald Canopy Lodge. It's dated over a month ago. I open it enough to see a sticky note, with handwriting—not Hollands, that says, "Appreciate the discussion. Let us know what we need to do to move this forward."

My hand hits my chest as I drop the paper, like it's going to burn my fingers, on the counter. Air is hard to grab, but I do my best to breathe—all I can muster is something shallow and not satisfying. The fingers on my chest feel my too fast heartbeat. A wave of lightheadedness hits me and I furrow my brows, trying to figure this out. Instinctually, I step back, trying to put as much space between me and what I just read.

What is happening?

There's no way Holland can sell the lodge. It's always been owned by the Holt family. Why would Holland step in, after everything with Hazel, just to turn around and sell it? This is what's left of his sister; he can't honestly be considering selling it.

Right?

The only thing I can see from here is the date, like it's taunting me. My brain calculates the amount of days between now and the date and that's all I can see in my tunnel vision. It's not like there weren't discussions or meetings before a formal offer. This has been going on for longer than that.

How could Holland keep this from me? For this long?

I live here. In this house. Part of the lodge. What happens when Holland sells it? Where do we go? Wait, is there still a "we?" Maybe Holland has had enough and this is an exit strategy. Has he figured out that I'm too much?

I know I'm spiraling but being aware and stopping it are two different things. Tears cloud my vision. I try to swallow but it's like my mouth is full of sand. I reach for my cup of coffee and take a drink. Setting the mug down, harder than intended, Slate runs in, as if he knows something isn't right.

It's not.

This is wrong.

CHAPTER ELEVEN
Holland

I'm trying to be productive but the thought of keeping Ivy in the dark with potentially selling the lodge, and having her home, has me in knots. I can't find my flow and this morning has been nothing but frustrating.

"Did you and Bailey decide on a time for the Wildflower Fiction pop up?" Bea asks, standing in the doorway of my office.

"Where's this coming from? Who is asking?" I can feel the tension in my shoulders, muscles tight in my upper back.

Bea puts her hands up in surrender, taking a single step back, eyes wide and looking at the floor. "Just me but I don't think it's worth it." When she does make eye contact, the wave of guilt hits hard. This has nothing to do with Bea and everything to do with me. I'm on edge. "I don't need new stickers or a book that bad."

"Fuck, I'm sorry." I put my head in my hands, running my fingers through my thick, dark hair.

"For snapping at me or your general bad attitude?" She crosses her arms and I know she's ready to go toe to toe with me.

"Both?" I wish it wasn't a question.

"What is going on? I thought this dark cloud of whatever is happening would go away when Ivy was back home, but you're just as moody as ever." She walks into my office, closing the door behind her.

"It's this thing. This thing I've kept from Ivy and—"

"For the love of everything, do not tell me whatever it is. I don't want to know." Bea says, shaking her head, making sure I hear and see her "no."

"I won't tell you," I say because at this rate, she's about to run out of here backwards, straight into the front desk area. "I've been wanting to tell her for so long but every time I get close, there's something else. Then it was the event. She's been so stressed."

"If you think you can manage Ivy's stress, you're in worse shape than I thought. That woman is a force and she has shown you, time and time again, she can take care of herself."

"You're right."

"Of course, I'm right." She throws her hands up in the air before setting them on her hips. "Holland, secrets are usually never good. Especially ones that make you feel like this." She gestures to me.

I know she's right. This is self-inflicted and I'm hating myself for letting it get that bad. It's clear I need Ivy to help me make this decision. There's not a lot I know about the future, but I know the only thing I've pictured has Ivy by my side.

"Now, quit pretending like there's anything important here that needs your attention. There's not. You need to make this right with Ivy." She might be wearing a headband with pink flowers on it, but there's nothing light and playful about her right now.

"Don't sugar coat it, Bea."

"Not when it counts, Holland. Ivy is too important." She says it like it's a fact and known to everyone. That's the thing about Bea, she's tough but always finds a way to get rid of the murky feelings clouding my brain.

"Do you need anything before I go?" I start gathering my things, putting on my jacket, eager to get home.

"No, but make sure to keep an eye on the weather—"

"I saw the potential ice, shouldn't be too bad."

"Quit interrupting, especially when you don't know what you're talking about." Her voice is sharp like a razor blade. "Snowstorm is coming. They're predicting blizzard conditions. We're getting extra supplies and going through our storm plans, so we should be all set here."

Blizzard? Naturally. Can never have just one thing crashing and burning.

"Okay, call me if you need anything. I'm going to go home and get this figured out with Ivy." I'm already out the door, talking to her over my shoulder.

The rain outside hasn't let up and the temps continue to drop. I open the door to my truck and a wind gust—the kind that bites your cheeks—hits at the same time, feeling like it's going to make the door fly off.

Once inside, I'm happy to be buckled in, shielded from the elements, and making the short drive back home. How I'll bring this up to Ivy consumes my thoughts. I try to imagine how this will go, how she'll take it, what I'll say.

Before I can get lost in my thoughts, I see someone walking on the side of the road. This is common for most days, but I didn't expect to see anyone out here with the weather like this. Rain drops fall heavy and fast, my windshield wipers struggle to keep up.

I slow the truck and roll my window down. When I'm almost right next to the person, I see they're wearing pink rain boots. My mind finally connects the dots. This isn't a random lodge guest; it's Ivy. Immediately, I stop the truck, put it in park, and get out.

"Ivy, what the hell are you doing?" She's walking towards me, eyes focused on the ground in front of her. Her hood is down, I'm guessing the wind made it impossible for it to stay on. Her hair, usually a soft brown, looks jet black as it's soaking wet.

Her eyes snap to mine. "Me? What the hell are you doing?" She bites back.

I grab her by the shoulders, "What are you talking about?"

She steps back, giving herself room, and unzips her pocket. When she pulls out the folded paper, I know I'm in trouble. The offer papers. *Fuck.*

"You're selling the lodge? What is wrong with you?" she yells out of what I'm guessing is anger, and the wind makes it hard to hear.

"I might be selling the lodge. Nothing's been decided," I say, taking a step forward. Ivy holds the papers out so I grab them.

"Why should I believe you?" she shouts, stepping back. My heart hurts with the space she's putting between us. "This is an offer, an actual proposition to buy the lodge. You never said anything." Her voice goes from angry to sad and it's breaking me open. "You've had this for over a month."

A wind gust blows through and Ivy puts a hand up in front of her eyes, shielding them.

"I was going to. I swear—"

"When were you going to? When I had to pack my things? When you started a new job?" Her voice is sharp and cuts through the rain and wind.

"Fuck. It's not like that," I reply, but as I say the words, I hardly believe them myself. I know this looks bad, probably worse than what I imagined. The anxiety I felt earlier in my office is back, stronger than ever, flipping my stomach and invading every inch of me.

Ivy shakes her head, a sarcastic smile painting her lips.

"We need to talk about this but we need to get out of the road," I look around, thankful there's no one else around.

When Ivy crosses her arms, putting weight on one leg, and stares at me, I know I fucked up. I mean, I knew it before this, but seeing her like this shows me the severity. She's soaked, standing in the pouring rain—her lip trembles with tears or the cold. Maybe both.

Long seconds pass before she walks over to the passenger seat. When she gets in, she doesn't look at me.

Fuck.

We drive the short distance back home. As soon as I put the truck in park, Ivy's hand is on the handle, and she's already half out.

I take a deep breath and rest my head on the steering wheel, just for a second. I'm trying to figure out what to say first, when it's just her and I inside. No wind or rain to fight with.

As ready as I'll ever be, I open the truck door, fighting the wind, and what is now ice, all the way to the front door.

Once I'm inside, I see Ivy on the leather couch. Eyes on her hands, which sit in her lap.

It's not much better in here than it is outside.

CHAPTER TWELVE
Ivy

If it wasn't for the panic and anxiety running through my body, I'd be freezing. When I made the split-second decision to walk to the lodge and confront Holland, I didn't account for the weather—ironic considering that's a key part of my anxiety. In hindsight, I needed more layers and a hat that would stay on, no matter the wind.

Now, I'm on the couch, my hair soaking wet. I pull the brunette strands into a bun, not wanting to drip all over this leather couch, which I've always loved. I wipe my hands dry on my shirt, before setting them in my lap. Slate ran over to me the second I walked in the door. I pick him up and he sits down next to me, touching the side of my thigh.

The cold in my fingers makes them almost numb, something I didn't notice until now.

Holland pauses in the doorway, the door slammed shut by the wind. I don't look up because I'm afraid I'll just keep talking. Questioning. It's Holland's turn. I focus on my fingers, rubbing them together, keeping my eyes down.

Holland takes a blanket out of the basket on the side of the couch and wraps it around my shoulders before he sits in the chair across from me.

"Ivy, I'm sorry. I kept trying to bring it up and it never felt right," Holland says as I keep my eyes down, even though I know that's now how people effectively communicate. Sometimes, I want to be a little childish and stomp my feet. This is one of those times.

"No decisions have been made, honestly. This is an offer and I've envisioned saying yes but also saying no. But the more I thought about it, the more I knew this wasn't a decision just for me. It's for the both of us."

I look up to see his dark eyes fixed on me.

"Hard to contribute when I didn't even know this was something you were considering." Again, I know it's not super productive but I'm being honest.

"I know that. And it's not like I searched for these people. They stayed at the lodge and approached me. I've had three meetings and nothing is set in stone."

"Why are you even entertaining the idea of selling?" I ask, trying to give no information on my own insecurity.

"This company has success in making places like this thrive, not just for now, but forever. It's something that would help make sure the lodge can be viable for a long time."

"Is the business in financial trouble?" I ask, trying to understand. Holland and I rarely talk about business specifics but maybe that's because he's embarrassed. Maybe it's going under? Maybe it's sell the lodge or close it? My thoughts jump from one disaster to the next in the brief span between my question and Holland's answer.

"No, we're making money. Everything is okay. But it's not because I necessarily know what I'm doing. I feel like I've been lucky up to this point." Holland's voice is level and clear. If he's upset or agitated, I don't see it. "When I took this place over, it was because I owed it to Hazel.

All in the hopes of it being successful. These people might be able to do something I could never do."

He swallows something back, pressing his lips together.

"They might be able to preserve Hazel's vision. What she wanted for this place." His voice almost cracks and it hurts me.

The sincerity in his eyes tell me what I knew, deep down. This isn't malicious and comes from a good place. His execution desperately needs work.

"Holland, I get that. I just don't understand why you didn't tell me."

"There were so many times I almost did. But, you have had so much going on, and I didn't want to pile on. And then I thought when you came back home, after the event was done, we could talk about it."

"If you haven't noticed, I always have a lot going on. My job is sometimes unpredictable, plus I'm just that kind of person. If that means you're going to keep important things from me, I've found a serious flaw in our relationship." It's sharp but honest.

Yes, I've made lots of changes in the last couple years in therapy, but the work is never done. Plus, things you work through always seem to come back for more work later. It's part of the deal, which I'm fine with, but I'm nervous Holland thinks there will be a time I'm just "better," more together and with less going on.

"You do but this event is a new thing. I'm so fucking proud of you for doing it, even though it meant you spending extended time away from home. I was trying to support you through it and thought this could be an after thing."

Even though I'm disappointed, and still confused, Holland is doing his best to be clear and honest. I appreciate it.

Slate, wanting more of the blanket, walks onto my lap, curling up. The amount of serotonin this dog brings me is unreal. I'm immediately in a better mood, even if it's just a few notches.

"I know you meant well but do you know what I felt when I found these? One second, I'm looking for a pen and the next it felt like my world was slipping away. Like, maybe you didn't want this," I point between the two of us, "anymore." The last part flies out of my mouth before I can keep it to myself.

Holland stands up, coming over to the couch, a look of sadness etched on his face.

"Out of everything in the world, the thing I know I want is you. Forever. No matter where that is," He puts his hand on the nape of my neck, pulling me closer to him. When he rests his forehead on mine, his eyes, the color of honey, find mine.

"Ivy, I love you, and I'm sorry you thought that had changed, even for a second." He kisses me, his lips are soft and full. He keeps his forehead on mine.

Feeling his eyes on me, intense and full of love, soothes the panic a bit—pushes it further from the edge. Holland was in the wrong for not bringing this up sooner, but I know my brain contributes to the problem.

I typically overthink too many interactions: what I, or someone else, said or did, and intentions. But that's not the case with Holland. He's also the first man I've been with who doesn't make me question everything—it's one of the reasons I fell so fast. For once, I felt like someone saw me for me, and still liked what was there.

Holland is the space where my brain gets a break. Today is not typical.

"I know you love me." My voice is barely above a whisper and I lean further into his touch. "I'm sorry about the spiral, I was just so caught off guard." I sit back onto the couch, breaking our contact.

"Don't do that."

"Do what?"

"One, take responsibility for something you didn't do. That was something I did," Holland emphasizes with a hand on his chest. "Two, don't talk bad about your brain. It's beautiful and does a lot of great things."

I don't know what to say, so naturally, I start to laugh—my go to response. I cover my mouth with my hand like Holland can't see my shoulders shaking. A borderline uncomfortable grin pulls on his lips as his eyes grow bigger.

"What is happening?" he asks.

"Never heard someone tell me I had a beautiful brain," I giggle before I can cover my mouth. "It's like my brain can't compute the phrase."

"Here's what I think we should do," Holland stands, grabbing the papers from the ottoman. "I'm going to give these to you, plus the email thread from some questions I had. I want you to take the time to read and process what's here, and then we can talk."

"Woah, your therapy is showing." I try not to let my mouth hang open because I literally couldn't think of a better way to pause this discussion to make it more productive.

"I have some running around to do quickly. Not to freak you out or anything but looks like snow is coming. They always predict much more than we get but it's always better to be prepared."

My stomach drops. I recognize it's because I'm caught off guard.

"I'm going to check on the lodge and then I'll go to the store and be back here before you know it. Sound good?"

"Yes. Sounds good. Do you have another copy of this or is this like it?"

"I have the file in my email, so if you want to take it in the bath, completely fine."

I'm still upset about this whole thing but one thing is clear: Holland knows me, down to my bones.

It's hard to say no to a bubble bath.

CHAPTER THIRTEEN
Holland

ONCE I'M IN THE truck, I rest my forehead on the steering wheel. I need a few seconds.

I close my eyes and put my hand on my chest, needing to make sure I'm not going into panic attack territory. I felt much more confident when I was with Ivy, because my mind had something to do. Now, the interaction comes back in pieces—I don't fight it.

My stomach drops when I think of the look on Ivy's face, when she explained how finding those papers made her question if I still loved, or wanted, her. I hate that this is one of the first things she puts on herself when something like this happens. It's almost like a programmed piece in the woman I love, and in this moment, all I want to do is my very best to not ever put her in that position again.

No more secrets. Not only for her, but for me. This whole thing could end up being positive, but the way I went about it only made everything feel dark and like a potential enemy.

I take in a deep breath, hold, and exhale. The sound of the heavy rain, and what sounds like some ice, hitting the truck help me relax.

Ice. Fuck.

I open the weather app for an update. My phone screen turns red, the banner at the top scrolling with both a winter weather and blizzard warning. When I view the radar, it's obvious we'll get snow but it won't start for another few hours. I'm confident I have time to check in with Bea before going into town to get supplies.

I put the truck in drive as I head back to the lodge. Even if Mackenzie is all over this, I want to check in and make sure there's nothing I can help with.

One of the major upgrades Hazel completed at the lodge was for storms like this. She redid some of the electrical work, running it underground, to help keep power outages to a minimum. If it does go out, there's some ridiculously high-tech generators and things to keep the lodge powered, to an extent. There have only been a handful of times the power has went out, since I've taken over, and it was never for more than an hour.

When I walk into the lobby, I see Bea directing someone with extra blankets. When we get snow, we always hand out these plush, almost velvet, blankets to the rooms. Typically, it's an ambience thing, but if we get as much snow as they're predicting, we want to make sure everyone is comfortable.

"Holland, hope you have a sled for Slate!" she jokes as soon as she sees me.

"How's it going?" I ask, taking in the scene around me.

"Great! Mackenzie has the staff bringing in extra wood for all the fireplaces in the common areas. We did some rearranging, putting as many spots in those areas in case we do lose power," Bea says and I can't help but smile at the snowflake headband she's wearing.

"That's a really good idea," I reply as the staff moves around us, not panicking, but getting things done. I love that all of this started happening without me telling anyone to do it.

"We did an extra food run. Chef has been cooking, and baking, all day. Premade meals and snacks are ready, in case we need them," she explains and I breathe in the smell of fresh bread.

"Don't forget to grab all the cards and board games, put those in the shared areas." The worst part when anyone loses power is they don't know what to do with themselves. When their phones die, it's like no one knows how to act.

Bea nods and writes something down on a sticky note. "I think we're all good here. You ready at your place?"

"Going to town to get gas for the generator and grab some extra groceries. We've got everything else we need."

Bea comes over to me, out from behind the desk, and wraps me up in a hug. "You usually stay here with us, so make sure to let me know you're okay." She goes back to the desk, grabbing a radio, and handing it to me. "And, if you take Slate outside, I want a picture!" She winks before turning back to the front desk, like she has a thousand things to do.

"You got it, Bea. Please keep me updated, even if you and Mackenzie have it under control." I point at her, because I mean it.

Bea nods, giving a thumbs up, before her eyes are back down on her to-do list, getting to the next thing. While I walk back out to my truck, I stop. I'm standing in the rain, wind still whipping around, but I'm proud. The lodge is going to be just fine, no one was panicking, and they don't need me to make sure things are taken care of. It's a good feeling to build something like this.

I quickly get into the truck, eager for something to block the wind. Once the heat hits my face, I almost smile before putting the truck in drive. On to the next thing on my to do list.

CHAPTER FOURTEEN

Ivy

Bubbles fill the bath and lavender wafts through the air. I step one foot into the steaming water, sucking in a breath as the temperature is a shock to the system. When Holland left, and it was just me and my thoughts, the chill hit my bones, down to my marrow. My wet hair didn't help.

I lower myself into the bubble bath. The water, borderline scalding—just how I like it, reaches to the top of my chin. Everything, besides my head, is submerged. The bubbles touch my chin and ear lobes.

I rest my head on the back of the deep soak tub; it's ridiculously comfortable. I breathe in deep through my nose, hold for a count of four, and loudly exhale with my mouth.

Before I get into the offer details, I need to steady my mind and emotions. My therapist encourages me to make a list when feelings, or thoughts, are hard to sort.

What do I know, without needing any other information, to be true, at this moment?

First, Holland would never do anything to intentionally put the lodge at risk. The love and care he's shown this place, both the actual structure and what it means to the community, is substantial. I know how much this means to him and his family.

Second, ownership could mean quite a few things. I've been around for enough acquisitions and business purchases, in the wellness space, to know there isn't a one size fits all approach. From the brief explanation Holland gave on the interested party, it sounds like this is something they do and are good at.

Third, Hazel built this place, our home, and I don't ever see Holland giving this up. Even if he didn't work at the lodge, or sold it, or whatever that entails, I don't see a path where this place doesn't belong to him. Honestly, this is the last piece of Hazel; she poured so much love into this place.

Fourth, Holland loves me. This decision or proposition or whatever we call it, has nothing to do with the state of our relationship. It wasn't fair for me to jump to that conclusion and tie that insecurity to this.

Lastly, I love bubble baths. I feel like they give me the space for clarity.

I sit up, reaching for the towel to dry my hands, before grabbing the thing that changed the trajectory of today. It feels weird to hold this in the bathtub. The pages are crinkled from the rain, being stuffed in pockets, and my overzealous fingers.

I read through every page, not missing anything or skipping ahead. I'm not a lawyer, obviously, but this is written in a way that much of it is easily understood. Greater When Green has enough contingencies to tell me that they seem to be out for what's best for the lodge, and in turn, Holland.

Next, I pull out my phone to open my email. I read through the thread Holland forwarded. My thought of this organization being a good one is reinforced with the patience they've shown Holland and the extra information they've provided. No matter what question Holland asked, they always had an answer, or took the time to find one.

I learn that the offer I read through, wasn't put together until Holland had a meeting with them to share what was most important to him. It looks like, from the meeting notes, this is when Greater When Green explained the perks of ownership but it's clear they still want Holland, and the current staff, involved. All good signs.

But, here's the thing: once you sign on the dotted line, there's lots that can change. Many organizations promise lots of things but rarely follow through. However, this offer is written in a way that much of it would need to be attempted or done, or it seems like the deal could fall through.

Once I've taken in all the new information, I drink a full glass of water. Sweat beads on my forehead, the water still hot enough to have steam roll off it. I leave my phone on the side table, the one Holland bought once he realized how much I loved taking baths.

I sink back into the water, trying to sort through this.

MY FINGERS FEEL A little weird on my laptop trackpad—still pruny from the long bath. After I soaked for borderline too long, for my skin and my own thoughts, I needed to be productive. Now, I'm almost done reading through all my unread emails—a solid distraction. Unfortunately, my event 'ay of to-do list' is longer than earlier. For now, it seems like all the key pieces are taken care of and we're tying up loose ends.

Or, that's what I tell myself to make me feel better on the other side of the United States.

I do a weather check and see that there's significant snow coming. My flight back to New York isn't for two more days but I open the airline app to make sure everything is still on schedule. The green "on time" showing by my return flight has me exhaling a breath.

I close my laptop and the door swings open, revealing Holland carrying a bunch of bags. Slate runs to greet him until he feels the gust of cold air coming in from outside. He makes another trip and I'm curious what all he considers supplies.

"It's getting gross out there," Holland says as he brings the rest of the bags in and sets them on the counter. "No snow yet, but some icy roads. The temps are dropping quick." He pulls off his black beanie, his brunette hair all disheveled and cheeks red from the cold.

"What kind of supplies did you get?" I ask.

Holland starts pulling things from bags. "We've got gas for the generator, in case the power goes out. Plus extra groceries, batteries, bottled water, and then the real essentials." He rests his hands on his hips, golden eyes catching mine.

I watch as he pulls out a new blanket, a couple bottles of wine, bags of sour candy, and a puzzle. My face must give me away because then Holland explains, "When we were younger, if there was ever bad weather coming, my mom would always get us a new puzzle. It's a longstanding Holt family tradition."

My heart warms—like it always does—when Holland shares pieces of his childhood. I know it's hard for him to talk about what it was like when Hazel was around, but he shares stories like this every once in a while. It's a little odd to hear when we're sort of dancing around the fight we had earlier—the need to pick up the conversation hangs heavy in the air.

"I love that," I reply before putting my hands on the new blanket, feeling the plush fabric beneath my fingers. "Anything else we need to do?"

"Not really. Everything is good at the lodge and we should be all set here. I can make dinner and then we can continue our discussion, if that works for you." Holland seems unsure as he offers his suggestion, his voice trailing off at the end.

"That sounds like a plan," I say, as I start putting groceries away.

I still don't know what I'm going to say, so I'll take all the time I can.

CHAPTER FIFTEEN
Holland

DID I MAKE PEANUT butter bacon cheeseburgers for dinner? Yes. Was it because I feel guilty? Also yes. I know there's nothing I can do to change how this happened, but I can show Ivy all the ways I know and care about her.

We both sit on the leather couch, the new blanket across our laps. Typically, Ivy would practically be in my lap, but we both left space between us.

Ivy breaks the silence. "Is there anything else you want to share about this whole thing? Any reason you want to or don't want to move forward with the offer? Anything you meant to say and didn't?"

I take a few seconds, thinking about what she's asking. She's giving me the opportunity to lay all my cards out on the table.

"At first, I was skeptical. I truly didn't think I'd be interested at all. But, when I saw the amount of money, and how I'd keep this and the land surrounding it, that's when it changed. I wasn't lying when I said the lodge is doing well financially, but with that amount of money, that could change our lives."

"What about our life do you want to change?" She gives nothing away with her voice level and clear.

"It's not that anything is wrong with it, I'm just pointing out that it would give us the opportunity. We could travel. Find where we want to put our roots down. You could quit your job, try something new." I list the things that went through my brain when I saw the amount of money they were offering. That, coupled with my healthy savings, would go a long way.

"Do you think I don't want to work?" Ivy's brows are scrunched.

"No, I'm just saying it could be an option. You're good at your job but it's also stressful and demanding, plus there's just some baggage there."

"You're not wrong but I want to work. No part of my brain has ever really thought about not working. Especially with my set up at Sparks now, it's flexible and lets me take on as much as I want," Ivy reassures me. "Somedays the baggage is annoying but not enough for me to leave. Wouldn't that mean Jack and Royce won? I don't want them to win. I want to win." Her hand sits on her chest.

Fuck. How does she do that? She always seems to know exactly what she wants.

"Do you hate not having an office? I know there's not a ton of space here." I look around the space, the one I love.

"No, I've never wished for anything other than what's here. I love this space and it's perfect for us." She puts her hand on my leg, squeezing. "After reading through everything, I was much more relieved. Like, this is favorable to you, and the place you've helped thrive. I don't want to ever give this up. But if you want to give up some of the pressure, I'll support you."

"What would you do?" I'm looking for anyone to give me a tip, direction.

"You know I can't answer that. I'm here to contribute but this isn't a decision for me. Given you could stay at the lodge, working like you have been, and we could live here, that's what's important to me. What's important to you?" She asks in a way that I know she's not looking for a response but for me to think.

What's important to me? Ivy. Slate. Hazel's legacy, which is the lodge. My family. This just makes things more confusing because all those things play into the thing we're talking about.

"This isn't an easy decision and I'm sure you'll go back and forth. It looks like they don't want to connect until January. Is there a hard deadline?"

"No. They basically said they could give me as much time as I need, but to let them know the second I'm not interested anymore."

Just another reason I'm impressed with Greater When Green. They honestly have been supportive of me coming to a decision on the timeline that works best for me. I know that's not always the case.

"Okay, well, there's no need to try and solve it tonight, right?"

I agree with a nod, looking at my own hands in my lap. This territory is new. Ivy and I rarely fight, and not over anything like this. The room is heavy and fragile all at the same time.

"I also owe you an apology. Storming out of here, on foot, wasn't what I should've done. We both deserve more than what happened today." She locks her green eyes on mine. "You're right, I've been overwhelmed with this new event and I'm trying to be better at handling it." Her eyes dart around, as she fidgets her fingers in her lap.

"We'll both do better next time," I say before leaning in, putting my hand under her chin, and putting my lips on hers. Nothing feels better than when she kisses me back.

This conversation was so much worse in my head. I went back and forth about how it would go and I feel relieved, seeing where we ended up.

It's not perfect or completely resolved, but I don't feel like I'm being crushed with uncertainty.

"Come here," I say, putting my arm out, giving Ivy room to lay against me.

She picks Slate up, rearranging his sleeping position, before closing the space between us. Ivy wraps her arm around my stomach and puts her head on my shoulder.

A wave of warmth washes over me, like the sucker I am. Tonight, the three of us, together on the couch, is all I need.

CHAPTER SIXTEEN
Ivy

3 DAYS BEFORE THE RED CARPET EVENT

I wake up and the house is too quiet—pitch black. When I pull an arm out from under the blanket, I can tell it's much colder than it should be.

With a gentle shake, I wake Holland up. "I think the power went out."

He sits up, rubbing his eyes, taking in the room. "I'll go turn on the generator. Be right back."

As soon as Holland is out of his spot, Slate pads over, but this time he's trying to get under the blanket, which isn't common. I pet him, feeling the tips of his cold ears.

Grabbing my phone, I see that it's a little after four in the morning. I open the weather app to see the same warnings and calls for large amounts of snow. The only thing that's changed is that it's currently happening.

When I look at the radar, playing the projection for the next twelve hours, it's just the entire screen covered in blue. I have to watch it more than once to ensure the radar is actually moving.

It's only a few minutes before Holland is coming back up the stairs. He flicks the light on quick, probably to check all is well with the generator.

"Well, I've never seen this much snow since I've lived here," he admits while crawling back into bed.

"Really?" A pit forms in my stomach. I'm just not in the mood for record breaking blizzards or anything. "Is there anything we should be doing?" I ask, while turning towards him.

Holland picks up the blanket, confused at Slate, before getting comfortable, putting his hand on my hip. "Besides sleeping? No. Nothing to do." I stare at him and I think he feels it when he says, "They will get a hold of me if they need anything at the lodge. Bea texted saying they lost power, but the generators kicked on automatically and everything is okay there."

I was hoping the lodge would still have power but I feel better knowing everything is okay.

The wind blows and rattles the windows. I turn on rain sounds on my phone—it's still too quiet. With Slate pressed against me, his steady breathing, and Holland's heavy arm, I'm able to drift back to sleep.

IT FEELS LIKE THE sun is in our bedroom—that's how bright it is. I squint, trying to open my eyes, and all I see from the bed is white blowing by the windows.

I peel myself from the warm bed and walk over to a window. There's not much to see besides miles and miles of white. It's still snowing and the wind blows it as it falls, making it look like it's everywhere.

"How's it looking out there?" Holland asks, voice heavy with sleep. I look over to see him stretching. Even in the winter, he doesn't sleep with a shirt on. His muscles are always a *good* way to wake up.

"Very white. And cold."

I fall back into the bed and reach for my phone. My weather app tells me that it's still snowing, shocker, and that you should basically stay where you are. It's not like anyone could see a road anyways. Looking at the forecast for the next few days, the snow will continue, but the winds should die down.

A notification, from the airline, pops onto my cell phone screen: your flight has been canceled.

"No!" I borderline scream. Holland jumps because he must have been drifting in and out of sleep. Slate also pops up.

"My flight's been canceled. Not even delayed, but all the way canceled." I stand up and immediately call the customer service number.

AFTER SITTING ON HOLD for over an hour, frantically pacing the kitchen, it's final: I'm not making it back to New York tomorrow. The storm system is massive and is impacting almost the entire United States, in some way or another. Almost all of the flights are grounded for today and tomorrow. Actually, I don't think I'll be flying out for a few more days.

I'm going to miss the event.

I immediately FaceTime Stella, setting my phone up, using a full cup of coffee.

"Ivy, what a surprise. How are you?!" she says while propping her phone up in her office.

Before I can say anything, I burst into tears. Stella, like the sweet person she is, let's me cry for a few seconds and doesn't say anything.

I press the heels of my hands in my eyes, before trying to wipe the tears away. "I'm snowed in and there are no flights, and I'm not going to be able to get back to New York," I try to take a breath so I can keep going. "Like, they won't even let me schedule a return flight at this time. I have all these things—" I pick up my notebook showing the 'day of to-do' list.

"Ivy. Try and take a breath," Stella says.

I try but it just results in more crying.

"First, are you safe?"

"Yes. I'm safe. We have a generator." I look around the kitchen, not that I even know what I'm looking for.

"Is Holland with you?"

"Yes, he's upstairs."

"Okay, that's good. We're getting snow right now, but it's minimal. Looks like we'll get your storm in a few days, but luckily, that will be after the event." She offers me a smile.

"There were all these things I was going to do when I got back or before the event started. What do we do about them now?" I know I sound like I'm whining but I really need Stella to tell me what to do.

"Well, let's be honest, some of them may not get done, but that's okay. But, I'm sure we can find someone to help out. Do you have anyone in mind? Is there anyone who is up to speed?"

And then it turns on, a beautiful lightbulb. Vivian. She knows almost everything about this event. No idea if Stella will let this fly or not.

"Yes, but they don't work at Sparks," I test the waters.

"I mean, if they're willing to help and they know what's going on, I'll pay them under the table." Stella laughs, her voice higher, excited that we may have a possible solution.

"I have to call her first. Can I get back to you?"

"Absolutely." She claps her hands together, and then puts her hands on her desk, getting closer to the phone. "Ivy, you can't control the weather, this isn't one of your superhero movies. Don't beat yourself up."

I laugh at the superhero comment. She knows I love Spider-Man.

"I'm sad we won't get to experience this together. I know you have poured your heart into this and it's going to be amazing. We'll take lots of pictures," Stella says.

The tears come again and I put my head down, for just a second.

"Thank you, Stella," I try to get the words out but they sound jumbled with the tears. I end the video call and put my head back down on the kitchen table. The tightness in my chest doesn't let up but as soon as I can keep it together, I FaceTime Viv.

Viv answers with a, "What's wrong? Why are you crying like that?"

"I'm snowed in. There are no flights. I'm going to miss the event but I need your help with the last minute tasks. Stella said she'll pay you, if you're able to help." Tears run down my face as I look at Viv, who has her brows furrowed and face almost too close to the camera.

"Yes. Of course. I'm working at the bakery for a few hours today but I'll be free tonight, and all day tomorrow for the event." Another wave of disappointment hits me when I remember how we were going together. I gave her my plus one ticket since Holland wasn't going to make the trip.

"Ivy, I'm sorry. I know this is killing you," she says in a gentle voice that makes my heart ache for her, my best friend.

"Thanks. I know. It sucks but the best thing I can do is make sure everything goes off, perfectly, and hopefully we raise a ton of money for the charities."

"Send me your list, with notes, and I'll call you if I have any questions, okay?"

I nod in agreement, reaching for my laptop.

Being productive, or getting something done, always makes me feel better. I send Viv the list of tasks needing to be completed, as well as contact information for the vendors she'll be working with. Just to be safe, I forward her all of the emails regarding any of the tasks, in case she wants any context.

As I'm hitting send, Holland comes down the stairs, freshly showered. He stands behind me, and rubs my shoulders for a few seconds before putting a kiss on the top of my head.

"Is there anything I can do to help?" he leans down and says close to my ear. I lean back into his touch.

"Make me breakfast?" I suggest.

The panic from the last few hours is still running through my veins but it's not as loud. There's really nothing else I can do, besides support Vivian from afar. I know she'll get a hold of me if she needs anything.

"I can do that. Might be able to do one better. How do you feel about a mimosa bar this morning?" A sweet smirk pulls at his lips. "I always keep a couple bottles of champagne hidden away, for days like this." He opens a cabinet, pulling out a frying pan.

I bet it's because he knows I love champagne. This makes me want to cry even more, but I do my best to not.

"Days like this, huh?" I joke.

"I mean, any day with you is worth having champagne." He winks at me, and it's hard not to giggle. Holland's cheeks blush and I love him for it.

"Let's do it," I say.

And if I can't have champagne at the event, better have some while I'm snowed in with Holland. It only seems fair.

CHAPTER SEVENTEEN
Holland

I FLIP PANCAKES ON the gas griddle, while the bacon pops and sizzles. I'm almost done making breakfast and the next thing on my list is cutting up fruit for our make-shift mimosa bar. It's not something I've ever done, or ever mentioned, so Ivy's wide eyes when I brought it up wasn't super surprising. A mimosa bar is always a hit at the lodge.

We have two juice options—orange and cranberry—with strawberries and pineapple for a garnish. I found Hazel's champagne flutes, the ones she was gifted when she signed the paperwork to become the owner of The Emerald Canopy Lodge. Like Ivy, she loved bubbly wine and anything with champagne. My chest squeezes thinking about how her eyes sparkled when she opened the flutes up.

I pop the cork for the second bottle of champagne, the first already gone. I look over to see Ivy's face pink, the way it gets whenever she drinks. She's sitting with Slate looking outside the floor to ceiling window. We can make out the patio furniture by the tops of the chairs, but the amount of snow is startling. The official total is fourteen inches during the last twelve hours.

"Why aren't you working on that puzzle?" I ask.

"I can't find any more edge pieces! You're better at it than me." She laughs as I fill her empty flute with champagne, leaving a little room for juice. She chooses cranberry this time, and adds just a splash, before taking a long sip.

Slate gets up from the kitchen floor and lays in his bed in the living room.

"Guess Slate has had enough." She shrugs and then lifts her flute to me, in a cheers. I clink my glass with hers and take a sip of my mimosa.

Ivy sits back and starts to giggle. "I'm a little buzzed," she says, like it's a secret.

"Your face gives you away." I point at her cheeks.

"It does not!" She places her hands on her face, checking for warmth. Even if she can't feel it, I know it's there. "Oh my gosh, do you remember the first night I was here? And I fell in the shower?" She loudly claps her hands and doubles over in laughter.

How could I ever forget? A drunk Ivy, in my shower, and all I heard was a loud noise. I thought she had cracked her head open. But no, she just was in there, laughing her ass off, talking about how baby giraffes walk when they're born.

"I will never forget that moment in my life. You compared yourself to a baby giraffe."

Ivy keeps laughing; her shoulders shake, and it's contagious. We're both in the kitchen, taking drinks of our mimosas, trying not to spill. I can't even look over at her or I'm going to completely come unhinged.

"I wanted you so bad that night," she says, catching me off guard.

"Just that night?" I poke back, standing in front of her.

"You know I want you every night." She grabs my shirt and pulls me closer to her, wearing a devilish grin. Her green eyes are on me and my dick twitches in response.

I reach down, to under her arms, and pick her up. She laughs as she's on her feet. When she wraps her arms around my neck and kisses me, she tastes like cranberry juice. Her lips, soft, kiss me in a way that's hungry—feverish. I wrap my hands around her low back and she jumps up, putting her legs around my waist.

She laughs when I turn and then set her ass on the counter.

"Ooh, you're good at that," she says, while leaning her arms back on the kitchen counter.

"If we want to go down memory lane, do you remember when I surprised you in New York and we made peanut butter scones?" I step into the space between her legs, which are dangling in front of the cabinets.

Ivy throws her head back in a laugh. "Of course I remember. We had sex in my kitchen," she says, to prove her point.

I hook my fingers in the waist band of her leggings and start to pull them off. Ivy bites her lip and helps me take them off. Her panties, red and lacy, are on full display.

"Like what you see?" she asks. I love when she's like this—bold, confident.

"Like isn't the right word," I say as I find her mouth with mine. I then kiss from her jaw to her ear. Ivy moans when I find her sweet spot, the one she loves for me to kiss. I grab her legs and pull her a little closer to the edge.

Hitching one of her legs, I kiss from the inside of her knee, all the way up her thigh. I get to where there's only a little spot of skin before where her panties start and I switch legs, this time kissing down.

"I love when you tease me," she says, watching me with those fiercely green eyes.

I push my erection into her, letting her feel how much I love teasing her. After a few times, and hearing her whimper with each touch through her panties, I take a step back. Ivy's chest rapidly rises and falls, her breath shallow.

I put my hands on the tops of her thighs, before walking one hand to the edge of her panties. I look up to see Ivy watching me. Using a finger, I pull the lace fabric to the side and slip a finger inside, her arousal coating my fingers.

"These panties are awfully wet, Ivy," I say, teasing her in a way that I love.

"You should take them off," she suggests.

So, that's what I do. And then it's just her on our counter and it's torture to not be touching her the way I know she wants to be touched.

I take my mouth and put it close to her clit, and lightly blow. She groans as she throws her head back, still leaning on her elbows, truly an elite way to see her.

First, I slowly kiss the apex of her thighs, adding in a soft bite or two. She wriggles underneath my touch. I delicately rub the inside of her legs, getting my hands closer and closer to her entrance, but still holding out.

"I need more." She pleads like I don't know.

I pull back, blowing on her center, one more time, before I use my tongue. The second my tongue comes in contact, she lets out this half scream that is so hot. My dick throbs in response.

Having her sit like this, is the perfect angle for using my mouth and my fingers. I fill her with two fingers at first, matching the rhythm of my mouth on her clit.

She moves her hips, just enough, to get the friction she's looking for. I lick circles around her bundle of nerves, and she grabs my hair. I know she's close.

When I add another finger, she whimpers before saying, "Just like that."

I suck on her clit, while my fingers work, and she grips my hair tight, almost pulling. Keeping my head steady, I let her move the way she wants on my mouth.

Ivy tips my head just enough and she's coming on my fingers, my mouth. The sounds she makes are ones that are burned into my brain, so fucking hot and needy. I love making her come with my mouth. She tenses and throbs on my fingers, her hands still pulling at my hair, and I lick and suck until she's pushing my head away, too sensitive for me to continue.

Ivy is spent on the counter, breathing heavily and still leaning back on her elbows. I hover over her, holding my weight in my arms, but lowering far enough to kiss her mouth. Her tongue teases me and my erection presses into her.

I pull my pants and briefs down as Ivy stares at me, and if she keeps looking at me like that, I'm going to come with any sort of contact. She sits up and I slowly press my dick into her entrance; she's weak and sensitive after her orgasm.

I take my time with a few short and slow thrusts. When I slowly push all the way in, her warmness surrounding me, she whines and pulls at my shirt. That sound she makes has me close to coming and we've just started.

Ivy sits up, wraps her arms around me and kisses my neck. When she bites my earlobe, I pick up the pace. My hands go from the counter to her low back, itching to go deeper, have more traction.

"That, ugh, it feels so good," Ivy moans in between kissing me and it's the encouragement I need. I thrust harder, faster, and I'm groaning as I teeter on the edge. She takes one hand and scratches down my back, and even through my shirt it feels so fucking good.

I take one hand and find Ivy's center. Her clit hits my hand every time I thrust and she moans. We hit our stride, and I'm about to come.

"Fuck, I, I might come again," Ivy cries out as she kisses me and moves her hand that was on my back into my hair, pulling. I make sure my finger is still hitting her center with each time I drive into her.

When she lets out a scream and starts to throb on my cock, it's over for me. My orgasm hits me hard, and I yell into the kitchen as I spill into her. She grips and pulls me closer to her.

I don't stop moving until she's damn near horizontal on the counter.

CHAPTER EIGHTEEN
Holland

I watch Ivy, and listen to Slate, take an afternoon nap. Ivy's dark hair splayed on the pillowcase always makes me pause. Mostly, it makes me think about how this bed was empty for so long, how lonely I was.

Not anymore.

After our extracurricular kitchen activities, and finishing the second bottle of champagne, Ivy was spent. I know she's bummed about missing the event, but she's taking it like a champ. I'm proud of her, but it still hurts to know this is breaking her sweet, planning heart.

Careful not to disturb them, I slowly get up from the bed, checking over my shoulder before I go down the stairs. I have an idea, one that needs both Viv and Bea. I put on my winter coat and boots—needing to check on the generator—and go outside. I don't want Ivy to overhear me.

The wind is dying down, but there are still strong gusts that come and go. The snow steadily falls, nothing like the overnight pace though. My teeth chatter as I look around, the snow sparkling around me. Hazel would love this.

First, I call Bea.

"Want to help me with an Ivy surprise?" I ask, knowing it's the best way to catch her attention and not have her launch into something random. She always has a story to tell me.

"You know I always do," she says, quiet in the phone, like she's telling a secret.

"Ivy's not able to make it back to New York, so she's missing the event. I'm thinking we do something at the lodge at the same time. We'll need the guests, the chefs, anyone willing to help."

"Perfect! People are getting a little stir crazy here. They'll love it." I love how enthusiastic she gets.

I share what I'm thinking, giving her enough direction but knowing she'll put her own spin on it, which is exactly what I want.

"Holland, this is going to be so fun! I'm surprised you came up with it to be honest." Bea's voice sounds a little skeptical as she delivers the backhanded compliment.

She's not wrong. Ivy always gives me more ways to even surprise myself.

"You're so nice to me, Bea." I poke her back. "I'm going to coordinate with Vivian, but I'm sure she'll reach out to you."

"Yes! We'll get going on this today and I'll keep you updated." Bea hangs up before I even have a chance to respond. Guess she's excited.

Peeking at the windows, I look to see if anyone is moving around inside. When I don't see anything, I call Viv, hoping Ivy is still asleep.

Vivian answers the phone with, "Is everything okay? Also, I've been texting Ivy and she hasn't responded."

"Yes, everything is good. I entertained her with a mimosa bar and she's taking a nap."

"Good god, that's adorable," she says in the flat way that if you didn't know her, you'd think she was making fun of you.

"I'm trying to do something for Ivy, since she's missing the event tomorrow. I think you'll be able to help, well you and Bea."

"If Bea's in, I'm in!" she says before I can even share any details on what I'm asking. "I do need to get a handle on this to-do list Ivy gave me, but I think I'll be able to knock most of it out no problem."

I tell her my idea and when Vivian gasps, I know it's a good one.

"Are you fucking kidding me? This is genius!" Viv says, a much better compliment than what I got from Bea.

A wave of excitement hits me, now that Viv and Bea are both in on it, and it feels like something we might be able to pull off. "Do you think it'll work?" I ask.

"For sure. Let me check with the event team at the venue, and I'll coordinate with Bea. Talk soon!" She hangs up, again, before I have a chance to say anything else.

I stare at my now-blank phone screen and shake my head. Viv and Bea are kind of the same person in a lot of ways. Before I get too reflective, a wind gust hits and puts snow in my eyes, also flying into my coat where it wasn't zipped, like around my neck.

I hurry inside, closing the door, and Slate barks from upstairs.

CHAPTER NINETEEN
Ivy

Being snowed in isn't that bad. Breakfast, late morning mimosa bar, drunk puzzling, kitchen counter sex, and a nap? I mean, I can't complain. Or, that's what I tell myself when I think about how disappointed I am about not getting back to New York.

Even though I'm disappointed, I'm trying to separate the feelings of gratitude. Holland has gone out of his way to try and keep me busy, whether it's with an orgasm or an indoor activity, and I'll never forget that.

Plus, he's basically cooked the entire time we've been stuck inside. Last night, he made one of my favorite recipes of his: homemade macaroni and cheer with toasted breadcrumbs. I love the way he looks when I compliment him on his cooking; I know he loves hearing it.

I open the door out to the patio, careful not to have a bunch of snow fall in. Earlier this morning, Holland shoveled and cleaned up the snow so we could sit out and have our coffee. We had to wear hats, scarves, mittens—the whole getup—but it was stunning. I'm still not a big outdoors girl, but seeing the snow like this, it's something the city doesn't have to offer.

The snow has stopped for now and the road crews are starting to plow and get the roads drivable. Holland was able to help out, with paths around the lodge, with his four-wheeler—a man of many talents.

I got an email from the airline saying flights are expected to resume tomorrow. I'll book a flight after chatting with Holland, but he's been so busy, running around all morning.

Slate comes up to where the snowy patio starts and smells around. He's still not sure what to do with all the snow. He keeps testing it with a single paw, but then holds it up like something gross is on it.

Holland opens the door, shaking to get the extra snow of his winter jacket, before hanging it up. Slate runs to him as I close the door to the patio.

"I have an idea," Holland says, while taking off his gloves. "How about dinner at the lodge tonight? The power is back and things are about back to normal over there." His cheeks and nose are red from the cold.

"Sure, that sounds fun."

"We could even get dressed up, if you want?" he asks while taking off his winter boots.

"You want to randomly get dressed up? I mean, you know I'm in but, are you feeling okay?" Holland would prefer to live in jeans and a flannel button up.

"I'm feeling fine. I just know you're missing out tonight and the least I can do is put on a nice shirt and go to dinner."

"Oh! Can we bring Slate? Remember, he has that sweater!" I clap and ask way too loud. Last year, a guest left the gift for us, or for Slate, and we've not had a chance to have him wear it anywhere yet.

"Bea will love it. Yes, we can take Slate," Holland replies before opening the door, hitting his boots together to get the excess snow off before putting them back in the closet. He agreed much faster than I expected, but even Slate has mostly been stuck inside. We're all ready for an adventure.

I run up and kiss Holland on the cheek, his skin cold against my warm lips. He wraps his arms around me, resting on my lower back, before reaching down and putting his chilled lips on mine. I try to move back, surprised by how cold they are, but he pulls me closer to him. I laugh into his icy kiss.

When he lets me go, I head upstairs to decide on what I'll wear. I'm sure Holland was doing anything he could to offer up a distraction, and I love him for it. Knowing he'll get dressed up, when we're just going to the lodge, shows how he cares about me. I'm grateful for this kind of love, all the days, but this time is a little extra special.

Even if today isn't what I expected, or planned for, I'm still feeling grateful for what it *does* look like.

△ △ △ △

WE'RE IN THE TRUCK, riding to the lodge. I keep looking at Slate in the backseat, because I honestly can't get enough of him. From here, it seems like he doesn't mind the sweater. I've already taken approximately one hundred photos—my camera roll is just rows and rows of Slate.

I smooth out my dress—a black Stella McCartney—the satin soft under my fingers. This is one of my go to little black dresses; it's mid length—hitting just below the knee—and has this wrapped top with blousy sleeves.

To complete a full-circle moment, I'm wearing the Manolo Blahnik heels I wore the first time I stepped foot into the lodge. I'll never forget making the walk from the car drop off to the lobby. Bea and I were fast friends, even though she kept calling me the click-clack-queen.

The snow has started to fall again, slow and almost sparkling, as it hits the road. I don't understand how someone could see something like this and still hate the snow. Granted, I'm not driving in it and I'll spend most of my night inside, but it's beautiful.

"What are your plans for the next few days? I need to figure out when I'm going back to New York to debrief on the event, and grab my stuff from my apartment." I look over at Holland, who looks good enough to eat.

Tonight, he's wearing this dark green Burberry dress shirt, with black dress pants. I bought the shirt, on a whim, when I was back in New York before moving out west. I was missing him so bad, doing some retail therapy, and when I saw it, I knew I needed him to have it. It reminded me of the trees and greenery surrounding the lodge.

He looks *real good.*

"Isn't New York getting the storm we just got?" he asks, but in a way that sounds like he already knows the answer.

"I think heavy snow is coming tomorrow but I'm not sure," I reply, looking over at him. His dark hair falls onto his forehead.

"There's time to figure it out. When the snow settles." He grabs my hand with the one not on the steering wheel and pulls it to his mouth for a kiss.

I could melt in this front seat.

Stella is texting me when Holland parks the truck. As I'm responding, he keeps looking at his watch, like he has somewhere to be.

"We're going to be late," he says, opening his door, one foot out before I can even unbuckle my seatbelt.

When Holland opens the back door, putting Slate's leash on and helping him down, I ask, "Late for what? Our casual dinner?" I scoff at him.

"You'll be late for the surprise," He replies, his eyebrows raised, and his
mouth pulled into a mischievous grin.

What surprise?

What is going on?

CHAPTER TWENTY
Ivy

DAY OF THE RED CARPET EVENT

We walk, hand in hand, through the mostly empty lobby—even the front desk is abandoned. Anyone who is out and about, offers me a smile and Holland a nod. It's like they're all in on some inside joke. When my heels click-clack through the empty hallway, I'm bummed Bea isn't around to hear and make fun of me for it, just like she did during my first visit. Even now she'll sometime call me the click-clack queen.

Holland stops me at a set of closed doors, outside the main ballroom.

"Are you ready?" he asks, smiling at me, looking from my eyes to the doors and back again.

"For what?" I still have no idea what I'm about to walk into.

He clicks his tongue before saying, "You'll see."

Holland opens the door and the ballroom glows. Twinkly lights hang from the ceiling and around the room. Tables set up throughout the space have candles lit in different sized vases—many of the candles float in the water. The ballroom is full of what I'm guessing are guests and staff members, for whatever is planned.

"What is all this?" I ask, walking in.

Holland points across the room, "Look."

Something is playing, on a screen, from a projector. I move a few steps closer and realize it's a red carpet. *A red carpet.* Just as I'm about to turn away, I see someone who looks like Vivian walk across the carpet.

"That looked like Viv," I say, squinting my eyes.

Holland smiles, looking at me to the screen and back to me again. "It *is* Viv. It's a live feed from the red carpet and once everyone's done walking it, we'll stream the event."

My mouth hangs open and tears flood my eyes. My best friend comes back on the screen and waves, knowing I'm on the other end.

"How did you do this?" My voice is small and there's no way to hide the crack at the end.

Holland wraps an arm around my shoulder and pulls me close. "Bea and Viv really were the ones to make it happen, I just had the idea."

Bea sees me from across the room. She waves at me, and I feel a tear fall down my cheek. Her hair is pulled back in glittery clips—a perfect Bea accessory.

"I can't believe you did this." I turn to look at him and his caramel eyes make the lump in my throat impossible to swallow.

"Well, to be fair, the guests were getting a little stir crazy. We just let them go through the stuff we have for on-site events. They helped pull this off."

The room is simple but beautiful. Some guests are dressed up and some are in leggings and shirts—not sure anyone expected being snowed in or invited to something like this. For some reason, this makes me even more emotional.

I turn my crying face into Holland's shirt. My heartbeat feels like it's loud enough for everyone to hear.

"Hey, careful. This is *Burberry,*" he says in a way that's sarcastic but also serious. He made fun of me when I told him the brand. I think it reminds him of the past version of Holland: the finance guy in New York.

I look up and smile before meeting him for a kiss. This man. I'm a puddle.

"Time check. Holland, get Ivy a drink and grab a seat. It's almost go time!" Vivian says into the camera, I laugh at her bossing him around, even thousands of miles away.

I can't believe this. Any of it. The range of emotions from the last few days play in my head. To end up here, and not be totally missing out on the gala tonight, my heart is full.

People squeal about Slate the entire way as Holland leads me to a table and shows me to my seat. I'll have the best view in the house.

"I'm going to get you a drink and some appetizers." Holland kisses the top of my head.

Before I have a few seconds to take in the evening, Bea sits in the chair next to me.

"Tell me those are happy tears!" She hugs me and rubs my back.

"Obviously! This is amazing." I pull back, wiping tears, careful not to ruin my makeup.

She pats my hand in my lap. "You deserve it. I hope there's some hotties on the red carpet." She shimmies her shoulders before getting up.

I watch the screen and can feel the anticipation starting to build. I can hear more people, car doors shutting, and what I'm guessing are people arriving. The one thing that was meant to be a surprise was the A-list guest list for the red carpet. Stella insisted that was one thing I wasn't in charge of. She was right; even from here, I'm excited to see who will be there to support the charities and two great causes.

Holland sits down in the chair next to me, an old fashioned for him and a French 75 for me. I'm a sucker for anything with bubbly wine. I hear Slate bark and find him sitting with Bea while people are fawning over him. I totally get it.

I lean my head on Holland's shoulder and the lights dim.

"Want to make sure we can see who's on the carpet," he says quietly, his mouth near my ear.

First, some of the Sparks Wellness walks the carpet—Stella is wearing a black Chanel dress that is gorgeous. She waves at the camera and I wave back, even though she can't see me. It's a little embarrassing but I don't care. Next, the founders and boards of the charities being represented make an appearance, hitting all the right poses to get those good PR shots.

The crowd starts to scream when Theo Walker, an up-and-coming Aussie F1 driver for McAllister, stands in front of the camera. Based on the gasps heard around the room, I'm not the only one who knows who he is. The room quickly jolts to life—I join them in standing and clapping.

Is he kidding? He's wearing a navy-blue Tom Ford suit, his bare chest on display as the jacket dips down into a solid V. On anyone else, I think I'd make fun of them, but Theo is owning it.

"No man should look that good without a shirt on underneath a suit jacket," Holland says, taking in all of Theo.

Before Theo makes his way inside, he moves closer to the camera lens, "Wish you were here, Ivy," he says, with a wink, and I feel my cheeks get hot.

Guests clap and holler; they're loving this.

Before I can even register what's happening, Locke Hughes comes into the frame, and the room continues to buzz.

"Holy shit! That guy won a Masters. He has a green jacket," Holland says, eyes wide and drool almost falling out of his mouth. I can hear the same thing from the guests around us.

Locke stuns in a dark charcoal gray suit. He must be over six foot tall and it's like I can hear the panties dropping from here. He's a showstopper and knows it. There's something hot about a man who knows how to move on a red carpet.

"I did not expect that." Holland is still in awe at the professional golfer on the screen. "Do you know him?" he asks.

"We've not met and it's a shame." I jokingly squeeze Holland's knee, his eyes still glued to the screen.

Like Theo, Locke moves closer with a message. "Hey, Ivy," he waves. "Tell Holland there's a signed golf ball for him at your Sparks office. Someone said he was a fan."

I look over at Holland and it's like he's a statue. Frozen. Unmovable. I shake his shoulders and the entire room claps when they realize that Holland is sitting with me. I'm sure many of the guests didn't know who he was.

"I feel like I could pass out." He takes a long drink of his old fashioned.

My cheeks pinch from smiling. I know everyone walking the carpet gave a sizable donation to the charities and I can't wait to see what the totals are at the end of the night. The amount of good we'll be able to do is overwhelming in the best way.

Holland pulls me in for a kiss and then the room goes feral. People may have known who Theo and Locke were, but whoever on the screen has people jumping up and down, getting their phones out to take photos.

Tripp Owens and Willow.

"No way! There is no way!" I stand and scream, joining in the awe. Everyone claps and cheers.

Tripp, Super Bowl champion and MVP, stands in a timeless black suit with a blue pocket square—matching the blue of his team, the Upstate Cosmos. Willow, global-pop-superstar and my absolute favorite musician, wears a gold sequin dress which hugs her silhouette perfectly.

How in the world did Sparks pull this off?

I cover my mouth and watch as Tripp and Willow make me lightheaded with how sweet they are together. Tripp says something to Willow that makes her laugh, and even from here, you can tell she means it. They've been all over the media ever since they started dating, but I love how Tripp is a fan. There's the cutest video of him dancing, doing the actual tour choreography, while Willow performed the halftime show, and Tripp was supposed to be warming up. *Swoon.*

When the two of them walk forward, I reach for Holland's hand, and put the other on my chest. The entire room goes quiet, knowing what's coming next.

"Sorry to hear you're stuck out west. We were looking forward to meeting you," Tripp says as Willow gives a little wave. "I put you on the suite list for the next season. Anytime you want to see an Upstate Cosmos game, tickets are yours."

"Shut the fuck up," Holland shouts while looking at me. "Maybe we should move to New York," he jokes and I bump into his shoulder and "shhh" him.

"Ivy, I'm sure we'll cross paths when you make it to a game, but I left some merch and a couple signed vinyl records for you. Stella didn't know which albums were your favorites, so she checked with Vivian. If we didn't get it right, let me know. Hope to see you soon," Willow blows a kiss as she walks out of the frame.

I can't breathe. There is no air in this room. How do I continue after this?

Willow comes back, "Oh yeah, there's concert tickets in there, too."

The room erupts and I don't think my legs will hold me up much longer.

Holland stands and turns me to him, "Are you okay?"

"I don't know. I think I died dead just now." He laughs, hugs me, and I still can't compute what just happened.

"Looks like we'll have to make some trips to New York for those home games," Holland says while holding me.

"I guess so." I wonder if this is what shock feels like. I know every word to every song by Willow. I've been trying to get tickets to her new tour and haven't been successful. There are no words.

Not just for the thing with Willow and Tripp, but everything. Holland putting this together, Bea jumping in, Viv standing in for me in New York. It feels like I have all these people in my corner and that's not something I take lightly.

I sit down and take a drink of my French 75. Holland watches me, a smile on his face that could light this room.

"Thank you," I murmur. Tears are in my eyes, but no one is surprised.

"This was nothing. Just a good idea," Holland says, wrapping an arm around my shoulder.

I shake my head, "Not just this, for everything. You make my life so much better."

Holland tips my chin with his fingers, and catches my eyes with his. His caramel eyes on me, flip my stomach, and slow down time. It's like he's taking in all of me—every piece and flaw. Before Holland, this type of look would have me running for the hills, trying to hide parts of myself I didn't think were for show. With Holland, nothing is off limits. He doesn't judge and he loves me through it all.

He leans his forehead to mine, and says, "But then there's you. You, just, make my life."

And he kisses me.

CHAPTER TWENTY-ONE
Holland

TONIGHT WAS ABSOLUTELY PERFECT. I go to send Viv a text but before I can hit send, her message comes through. Great minds and all of that.

Vivian

How's our girl?

Me

Surprised. Weepy. Drinking French 75s

great cocktail.

I know it wasn't what she wanted but I hope she still feels part of it

you wouldn't believe the money they raised tonight

i'm sure she'll tell you all about it but she's happy

thank you for everything

no, thank you for taking care of my best girl

I smile and put my phone back in my pocket. I find Ivy sitting at a table with Bea and what looks like some guests. She throws her head back, laughing, and her drink is empty next to her.

First I go to the bar, get her another drink, and then I stop at the dessert table on the way back. You could've just called this the Ivy table because if this was for anyone, it was for her. My favorite sugar fiend. I fill the dessert plate with a s'more brownie, a piece of raspberry pie with oat crumble, and a classic chocolate chip cookie. These are some of our best desserts you can find at the lodge—you can tell because there's only a few of each left.

I walk to the table, careful to not spill the drink or topple the treats. When Ivy sees me, the look she gives me almost brings me to my knees.

Fuck.

As long as I have her by my side, I can probably do almost anything. The wave of hope runs over my body, unexpectedly. It's not often I feel this way because I'd basically convince myself I didn't deserve it. There's still moments where I don't think I do, but Ivy makes me feel like I can. I love her so much.

"Ooooh, treats!" Ivy exclaims as she sees the plate.

"The pie," Bea croons, giving two thumbs up. "That's the best one on your plate."

THE BALLROOM IS ALMOST empty. Someone's phone is plugged in and playing music across the space while some couples are dancing.

"Are you ready to get back? I'm sure Slate is," I say to Ivy, who is comfortably sitting back watching the few people on the dance floor, while Slate snoozes in his sweater in a dog bed we had at the front desk.

She nods, grabbing my forearm, wrapping her arms around it and leaning her head on my shoulder for just as a second. I grab Slate, bed and all, and head out of the ballroom. We pass a few guests in the hallway, everyone looking familiar and happy. Tonight was a win not only for Ivy, seeing her event come to fruition, but for the guests who've been stuck in the snow storm. Bea, Mackenzie, and all of the staff should be proud of what they've pulled off the last few days.

Slate is snoring as I set him behind the front desk—we'll just be a minute. I open the door to my office and check to make sure there isn't anything urgent on my desk. I can't imagine much would come in during the storm but want to be sure.

I hear the door shut and my eyes shoot up. Ivy stands, with her back resting on the door—her lips pull up in a devilish grin.

"What you did for me tonight. Amazing." She slowly walks over to the edge of the desk, her heels clicking on the tile floor just like that first day she strolled into the lodge. She rests her arms on the front of my desk, her perfect tits almost spilling out of her black dress with the way she's leaning forward.

"Amazing, huh?" I bait her.

She saunters over, slipping in between me and the edge of the desk. When she reaches out and grabs some of my shirt, pulling me close to her, my dick twitches. Ivy captures my mouth with hers and it's deliciously chaotic. It's lips and teeth, nibbles and swipes. She moans as I kiss her jaw and lick down the length of her throat until I'm at the top of her breasts.

"You don't want me to rip this, right?" I ask just as Ivy finds the zipper and pulls it down. She shimmies out of the top, the fabric falling down and baring her tits.

"Good girl," I praise her just how I know she likes it. She giggles and her cheeks turn pink.

We're in my office. My brain is about to short circuit.

My hands wrap around her lower back, lifting her up and sitting her on my desk. My very professional, but about to be fucked on, desk. When her ass hits the edge, her tits bounce, and Ivy lets out a sweet moan. She pulls her dress up and spreads her legs, giving me the space to stand between them as my cock touches her panties.

I take one of her nipples between two fingers and roll it. Ivy puts her head back, her breathing loud and raspy, before I even get my mouth on her other breast. I use my tongue to flick the bud before sucking.

Ivy takes her hand, running it down her body before reaching for my belt. I pull away from her breasts and watch unbutton and unzip my pants—my dick straining the fabric of my briefs. Then she has the audacity to lick her lips before biting them.

"You're fucking killing me, you know that? Fuck, everything you do drives me wild." I put my hands in her hair, pulling roughly and feeling her smile into it. *She likes it. That's my girl.*

Leaning myself into her, my erection hits her sweet spot and she groans. I kiss her and it's full of lust and need. I'll never get enough of her. Ivy pushes my chest back, creating enough space that she can run her hands down my chest and into my briefs. She strokes my length slowly, changing the pressure and direction. When she feels the bead of precum on the head, she whimpers. I move my hips, practically fucking her hand like it's my own. My orgasm builds, but I'm not ready.

I grab her wrist and remove it from my briefs. "My turn," I plead as I take a hand and run it from the inside of her knee, up her thigh, until I'm touching her soaked, lacy panties. I don't take them off, but pull them to the side and insert a single finger. She's fucking soaked.

"You're so fucking ready for me," I growl into her ear, biting her lobe, and nipping a few times down her neck, all while my finger moves inside her.

"More," she whines. I give her exactly what she's asking for when I insert a second finger, pumping in and out.

"Touch your clit," I demand. It's not a request.

Her hand immediately reaches into the top of her black lacy thong and does what she's told. The second her fingers touch her clit, she's moaning, moving her hips into my touch. I keep my eyes open, taking in as much of her as I can. Her dress all in disarray, her bare ass cheeks on my desk, all while she's touching herself. Fuck.

She sighs quick, breaths shallow,."I'm," she swallows, "close."

I take my hands and pull her forward, off the desk, and turn her around.

"Reach forward and spread those legs for me, baby." She listens so well and I can see her chest heaving, as her dress bunches up around the top of her hips, giving me the perfect view of her thong, and that perfect ass. An ass I fucking dream about.

Pulling down my briefs, I nudge her entrance with the head of my dick, but she's still wearing a thong. The lace is a friction I didn't know I needed. I play with her, lightly pressing my dick in, just a little bit, relishing the feel of the fabric.

"You're dripping. Going to make a mess in my office." I put my front to her back, letting some of my weight on her as I speak into her ear.

Then I pull my hips back and take my mouth to the top of her thong, biting with my teeth and pulling down, my lips touching her as I do it. When the thong is around her ankles, she looks back at me over her shoulder.

"You're going to touch your clit and I'm going to fuck you from behind. Don't stop touching yourself, or I'll stop." I love giving her orders because she's such a good listener.

She nods her head as I take my dick, and slowly fill her up. Ivy leans a little further forward, pushing her hips back, and I thrust in and out. The pace must be too slow for her, because her hips are trying to push back to meet mine, to get more, to take more.

I go torturously slow until she finally tells me what she wants.

"Harder. Please." Her voice is breathy and greedy.

"Well, since you've been such a good listener." I put my hands on both of her hips and drive inside her, using my hands to move her onto me, making my reach even deeper. One of her arms holds her up on the desk while the other works her clit.

Ivy groans, low and heavy, and I know she's about to come. I pump into her—hard and fast—and I slap her ass with one of my hands. A handprint quickly forms as the other digs into her hip. The sound of our skin and her wetness is all I hear, until she starts to whine and murmur with her climax within reach.

"Oh, fuck!" She borderline screams, her fingers still on her clit, and my dick pounding into her from behind. She contracts around me, the orgasm rising and falling just as I spill into her. I gasp and reach one hand for her shoulder, pulling her upper body up and back on my cock, creating a different kind of pressure as we ride it out together.

Slowly, I lean her forward and step back, pulling her thong back up. She turns to me, tits still out, skin red and marked from where I've kissed and bit.

"That," I kiss her cheek, "was fucking incredible. Just like you."

"I'm good at surprises too," she teases me, looking down at her tits that are still out.

"Yes. Very good." I can't take my eyes off her bare skin.

Ivy laughs and then throws her hands around my shoulders. "Best snowstorm ever," she says, and ends it with a sweet kiss.

EPILOGUE
Holland

"Are you sure that's going to be enough room?" I ask as Ivy and I stand over the blueprint in question.

"Yes, this will be enough room. Don't be a smart ass." Ivy lovingly taps my shoulder and our contractor laughs. "No other changes on my end."

Ivy is talking about the need to extend her office, or home library, another three feet to account for a specific style of built-in bookshelves she wants. It's not a problem, obviously, but it's fun to tease her.

Three months ago, I sold part of the lodge to Greater When Green. They're a 40% partner, for now, and I hold the remaining 60%. We're going to work together on a three-year plan that will bring Greater When Green resources to The Emerald Canopy Lodge. We'll re-evaluate in a year to see how it's going.

Honestly, I love working with Greater When Green. They're honest, transparent, and have great ideas that I've never thought of. Ivy comes with me to every meeting and we don't make any significant lodge decisions without consulting the other.

I love that she cares about the lodge as much as I do.

It was her idea to add on to our home. We'll be able to keep all the original work Hazel did but add on an office for Ivy. She's still working at Sparks but went down part time. Stella gave her a promotion—Head of Events. After the gala last year was incredibly successful and raised triple the funds anyone had even hoped for, it was clear Ivy had a different talent set they wanted to use.

Ivy loves it.

When she's not working at Sparks or helping me with the lodge, she works a couple hours a week at Wildflower Fiction. Her and Bailey hit it off at one of the pop-up events we did at the lodge and Ivy was practically drooling to work with the bookstore in any capacity. I love seeing the two women work together, they're unstoppable.

"If we want to beat the rain, we need to go now. " Ivy says. She's downstairs, getting ready for a walk.

"Just a second!" I yell down the stairs.

I reach under the bed and pull out a wooden box—I've had it since I was a kid. I've always used it to keep mementos and anything I wanted to keep safe. I feel for the dog collar and pull it from the box. There's a small compartment; you'd never see it If you weren't looking for it, but it's there. My fingers open it and pull out the ring—an emerald cut diamond on a gold band. The ring I've been hiding in this specially made dog collar, waiting for the right moment, to ask Ivy to marry me.

Today's the day. I let out a shaky breath but can't stop smiling.

After securing the ring safely back in the dog collar, I run down the stairs.

"Slate, come here. Got a new collar for you," I say while taking off the one he's wearing, that is in perfectly fine condition. I do my best to mask my trembling fingers.

"What's wrong with that one?" Ivy asks, referring to the gray collar with his name embroidered in navy blue.

Trying not to jump I say, "It's time for a new one, that's all."

"I like the gray better than the green," she says.

I clip Slate's leash to the new collar, holding on to the ring I'll use to ask Ivy to be my wife. "I doubt it," I murmur under my breath.

"Huh?" she asks. Guess I wasn't quiet enough.

"Nothing. Are you ready?"

She nods and smiles at me, before giving me a quick kiss.

I feel like electricity runs on my skin, knowing I'm just a few minutes away from our favorite look out point. The place I took her when we first met and she reached down, looping her pinky with mine. The place where I started falling in love with her.

Today, that place will turn into the spot where I get down on one knee and ask her to be my wife.

Here's to forever.

THE END

Acknowledgments

THIS ENTIRE PROJECT, THIS novella, is a dream come true. The fact that readers enjoyed *A Lodge Affair* enough for me to keep going? To write other books? To give you more Ivy and Holland? More Slate? More Bea? PINCH ME.

Bailey at Wildflower Fiction, for being the first indie bookstore to stock *A Lodge Affair*. You will never know what your support has meant to me. Thank you for making me feel like my books are good enough to be in a store like yours. I'm so proud of how far you've come with WF and can't wait to see where you are in another year.

Carly Robyn, for sprinting with me whenever the words are slow, and letting my include Theo as a cameo. YOU BEAUTIFUL BUT-TERFLY I LOVE YOU SO MUCH.

Grace Pearce, for cheering me on and letting me show off her grumpy golfer, Locke Hughes. LOVE YOU.

Mackenzie Wilson, for once telling me the funniest joke I ever heard and making it so easy to name a side character. <3

Stephanie, Rose, Jen, Kendra, for helping me with the earliest version of this thing. Your kind words helped get this to a place it deserved.

Keona, for always hyping me up and being the best PA ever.

Author friends like Ambar Cordova, Rachel Holm, Courtney Corlew, and Cleo White, for always making space for my questions, random rants, voice memos, and encouraging me that people *will* read my writing.

To every single reader who has picked up *A Lodge Affair*, this doesn't exist without you. You've changed my life, filled my head with fictional ideas and people, and made me find a way to write more books for you to devour. Thank you for treating me with such kindness and loving Ivy, Holland, and Slate the way I do.

Ruby and Rafa, for being the best dogs in the whole world and basically each being a half of Slate.

Lastly, my husband, Robby, for supporting me in this author adventure. Love you to the moon.

Want more of Locke?

Maren and Locke both exist in the same world of professional golf—he's the number one player in the world while she just takes his picture.

Never mind that Locke unintentionally leads the press to believe that he and Maren are dating, because when she confronts him, he couldn't care less.

Add in a reality show Maren is unfortunately a part of with her now ex-boyfriend, the number two golfer in the world, and she finds herself propositioning Locke to teach her how to quit caring...about everything.

Of course, Locke would never do something like that out of the goodness of his heart, so he asks for something in return—for her to accompany him to his pro-athlete obligations and to not take his picture. One thing they're definitely not doing? Fake dating.

But when their now 'fake friendship' starts to blur the lines, they both find themselves opening up to each other in ways they never would have imagined.

Want more of Theo?

The stakes this season have never been higher...

Josie Bancroft may be single, but she is definitely not ready to mingle. All she wants to do post-breakup is focus on herself. A simple task, but as a marketing manager for McAllister Racing, she spends every race weekend alongside the charismatic Formula 1 driver, Theo Walker. With his iceberg-melting smile and abs sharper than a cheese grater, he's a distraction she shouldn't entertain but can't seem to ignore.

Theo has mastered two things in life: winning races and wooing women. But this season, both are being put to the test. His team's new owner is threatening his hard-earned seat, and the one woman he wants has placed him in the friend zone, despite the fact that their attraction is hotter than his car's engine.

As Josie embraces her independence and Theo struggles to cement his place within the racing world, they'll have to decide if they want to fuel the flames of their friendship or forever wonder what could have been.

Drive Me Wild is a spicy Formula 1 romantic comedy with heart, heat, humor, and a guaranteed HEA. This is the second book in the Drive Me series and can be read as a standalone.

Want more of Willow and Tripp?

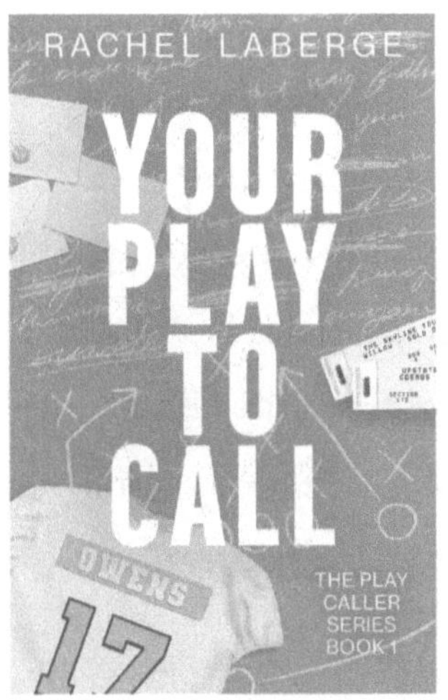

Global superstar Willow already has ten best-selling albums and sells out stadiums across the world, so how can she say no to playing the Super Bowl half-time show? She has to keep it a secret until the moment she takes the stage, but it's still a dream come true. When that secret proves to be the breaking point of her relationship, and Tripp Owens—the impulsive Super Bowl MVP—rescues her from the media, Willow retreats from the public eye.

At thirty years old, Tripp Owens has topped off his best football season by leading the Seattle Serpents to a Super Bowl victory. It's shocking, then, when he finds himself unexpectedly drafted to the brand-new Upstate Cosmos in the latest NFL expansion.

Months after that fateful Super Bowl game, everything has changed. Tripp is settling into his new team and new city, while Willow is hiding out, trying to convince her label a fresh musical direction is the best move for her career.

Once again, Willow and Tripp cross paths, but sparks flying between them wasn't in either of their plans. Ultimately, they have to decide if they want to play it safe, or if one of them will call an audible and change the play.

RACHEL LABERGE is the author of WHEN THE SNOW SETTLES. When she's not reading or writing, she's probably thinking about donuts, sour candy, or looking for her next hyperfixation. She lives in Michigan with her husband (Roberto), her two Frenchies (Rafa and Ruby), and cat (Riley). You can connect with her on Instagram, TikTok, and Threads **@rachellabergeauthor** (no 'R' name required).

Want to be first in line for updates and bonus content? Sign up for Rachel's newsletter at rachellaberge.com.

<u>**Other books by Rachel LaBerge:**</u>
A Lodge Affair
A Love Letter to Those Who Left Me Behind
Your Play to Call